REBECCA DINERSTEIN KNIGHT is the author of the novel and screenplay *The Sunlit Night*, and a bilingual English-Norwegian collection of poems, *Lofoten*. Her non-fiction has appeared in the *New York Times*, *Guardian*, and the *New Yorker* online, among others. She is a graduate of Yale and the NYU MFA program, and has received a Wallant Award for Jewish Literature. Born and raised in New York City, she lives in New Hampshire.

HEX

Rebecca Dinerstein Knight

BLOOMSBURY PUBLISHING

LONDON · OXFORD · NEW YORK · NEW DELHI · SYDNEY

BLOOMSBURY PUBLISHING
Bloomsbury Publishing Plc
50 Bedford Square, London, WC1B 3DP, UK
29 Earlsfort Terrace, Dublin 2, Ireland

BLOOMSBURY, BLOOMSBURY PUBLISHING and the Diana logo are trademarks of
Bloomsbury Publishing Plc

First published in 2020 in the USA by Viking, an imprint of Penguin Random House LLC
First published in Great Britain 2020
This edition published 2021

Sincere thanks to agent Jenni Ferrari-Adler, editor Allison Lorentzen, editorial assistant
Norma Barksdale, horticulturalist Michael Gordon, chemistry adviser Mika Efros, and
first readers John Knight, Jenny Slate, Michael Clark, Laura Bennett, Liz Fusco, Julia
Pierpont, Julie Buntin, Rachel Rose, Henry Walters

A catalogue record for this book is available from the British Library

ISBN: PB: 978-1-5266-1142-0; eBook: 978-1-5266-1144-4

2 4 6 8 10 9 7 5 3 1

Designed by Cassandra Garruzzo
Set in Warnock Pro
Printed and bound in Great Britain by CPI Group (UK) Ltd, Croydon CR0 4YY

To find out more about our authors and books visit www.bloomsbury.com
and sign up for our newsletters

This book is yours, my witch;
read it and you will find your tormented soul,
changed and free

VITA SACKVILLE-WEST

SEPTEMBER

Sometimes a banana with coffee is nice.

CLAIRE-LOUISE BENNETT

I AM A WOMAN WHO WAKES UP HUNGRY. TOM TOUCHED ONLY coffee till noon. You do what you're capable of at some point, so Tom and I left each other. I wanted breakfast, he wanted liberty, and who could blame either of us. I live alone now in a large rancid blown-out loft in outer Red Hook, where I pad around the soft wood floors like a toddler: I've taken my pants off, my rings, earrings, it is quiet and bright, I haven't gotten any lamps, I can hardly move, I'm drunk and I take a probiotic. My name is Nell Barber. I'm five foot five and 130 pounds which is not in any way remarkable. My daddy was a nice Jewish boy who married a nice Christian girl and raised me in Kansas and got on with it. Neither of them observed anything ever again. I was born observant. They gave me the original, fearful, organized minds of their childhoods and no religion of my own to honor. I suppose I turned from the celestial to the dirt. I study plants and I live in order.

Just because Rachel Simons made sustained contact with thallium and absorbed its toxins through her potassium uptake channels and died, the university expelled all six members of our lab. They couldn't tolerate another ounce of our hazard! The disciplinary committee stood in choral formation and issued what sounded like whale tones run through a vocoder. *Be-gone, be-gone*, they groaned. Our experiment in toxicology had taken the life of a valued graduate student and would no longer be institutionally condoned. I wore a hazmat suit to the hearing, to promise future caution. The chairman found this disrespectful and I could hardly see his apoplectic face through the scratched plastic front of my secondhand helmet.

Columbia couldn't accuse us—Rachel had oxidized the thallium of her own volition, at her own risk, and to her own demise— but it could close down the environment in which she'd endangered herself and rescind our schoolwide welcome. We had broken the contract of care and common responsibility that characterized the Columbia student. If we couldn't study safely, we couldn't study. It made good sense but it deleted me. The finalized verdict came via a specially assembled summer committee, via Priority Mail, to Tom's address, which I'd just kissed goodbye without any tongue. August is supposed to be a lazy month but it pummeled my partnership and my PhD.

The biggest loss is you: my chime, my floorboard. You are my night milk. You are my unison. You believe in the periodic table. Your book sold eight thousand copies in its first week. Columbia will separate you from the Simons case and nurture your celebrity. For five years I have been your smaller self, your near-peer, your sane challenger, your favorite. For five years I've trailed you as you approached success. Then Rachel reached for the rat poison and *Whole Thing* reached its readers and my room lost its pillars in one coordinated catastrophe and neatly fell down. You and Tom have both conclusively shaken me. Look, Joan, I'm shaking.

Tom and I lived in a rectangle of jewels, his mother's. A small palace they called an apartment on the Upper East Side, a good all-weather walk across Central Park to the university. Each morning

I'd emerge from that snow globe and enter the open air feeling forward-moving and weightless. Each morning I'd be a beetle creeping over the park's grass blades without bending them, so light was I. Now, when I step onto Van Brunt, my entire body weight rests on the sidewalk, but only and exactly my weight, not lifted not burdened. I've returned to my skeleton's original fact. If you asked whether I like it, I think I'd tell you I do. When you climb out of something you're very deep inside, the daylight is first a blank, and then it reveals itself to be life as you knew it before you climbed into that thing.

Everything has come around. Against the huge solitude of my schoolwork came the romance of Tom; against the romance of Tom came our utter lack of sex; against our nonsexual partnership came our easy, childlike living together; against our shared life, now, again, huge and unschooled solitude.

How undercutting, how generous of the world, to provide each thing with its inverse, to test each version of life we choose with a vision of its opposite. How perverse, and unpeaceful. I want more than anything to love the choice I make. Love it with abandon, proudly, building a temple upon it. But how can you do it, how can you really give yourself up and praise anything, when the world is too balanced to allow for a lopsided devotion, when each thing is always reckoning with its anti-self? Perhaps they're all the same, your various choices, and committing to one is the same as committing to any. Your only job is to build a temple.

In memoriam to the temple torn down, to my years of studiously laid bricks kicked over, to a classmate and all her skin, I close the old books and open this one. These savage castor beans and monkshood seeds are no longer the lab's property. Rachel's experiment is now my own; I can destroy it or it can destroy me, as I please. I please! As with the old work, the new work is for you, Joan. What isn't for you? More life collected, documented. You'd like that, wouldn't you like that?

YOU

YOU DUSTED THE EDGES OF YOUR SHELVES AS I PICKED SCRAMBLED eggs out from under my fingernails. I had expected to find your office swarmed. Being alone with you now felt supersonic.

"So what," you said.

"Well, the whole what," I said, wanting you to comfort me.

You hate comfort and I know that. I watched the end of your braid fuss against your collarbone.

"I have nowhere to work," I said.

"Work anywhere."

"I have no control, therefore I have no experiment."

I had to speak clinically in order to speak passionately. At the rate we were diverging, I soon wouldn't be able to speak to you at all. A mouse shot out from under your desk and seized the inch-long cylinder of string cheese you'd cut for it.

You clapped your hands once in satisfaction. Then you looked at me and forgot the success and moved down to study the gray, claw-footed saltcellar now resting emptily on your floor. The day flew in at us through your closed window. I wanted your inch of string cheese.

You said, "You have cold and temperate environments in your own home."

I said, "You have cold and temperate environments in your own intestines."

You blinked at me maliciously as if your eyelids could slap my cheeks.

"That lab was only extracurricular," you said, emphasis on the *ric.* "I let you play with it because you're a slobber toddler who needs a toy. What are you telling me—you're changing fields now to what, to botanical toxins?"

"I'm trying to neutralize botanical toxins."

"I thought you were generating a fossil-calibrated phylogeny of the American oak."

"No department in the country needs an oak specialist."

"What do they need?"

"Healed evil."

You made a face, a sanguine, unruffled pout. Your boredom made me cringe. I knew your every cue so well I might have become a bacterium in your gut. You coughed into your hand. I missed you and saw you changing into someone I would lose.

"I'll keep to my work and you keep to yours," you said.

"I need pizzazz," I said to your carpet. "I'm no star."

"Your oak work was reliable."

"I have to blow minds to keep up with you, Joan."

You looked at me as if I'd invited myself to your house. I looked at you as if through a screen door.

"Forget the oak work. I want to do Rachel's work. Doesn't somebody need to do it? We're just going to let her die?"

"She died, Nell."

"I'm saving her soul." What I didn't tell you is that I should have saved her life. That I go to bed at night certain her soul is going to grab my soul by the neck and strangle me from the inside out, because I was standing next to her and did nothing, and because why should I be allowed to keep living? "I've advanced her methods," I said, to stay on your track. "I think if I keep it going, I could speed up the disarming of poison to a rate that would almost undo the fact of the poison in the first place. You would call me The Great Undo."

"I never call you."

"And even if I kept on with the useless oak thesis," I said, "which I'd only do to satisfy *your* soul, your majesty," I curtsied, "I no longer have a school."

"That's your current problem."

You rank problems as current, finished, or irrelevant; it usually makes them smaller. This one didn't shrink.

"They expelled you precisely to stop you from continuing Rachel's work," you said. Action verbs like *expel* aren't spoken in Kansas and my shame swelled. You leaned toward me without any tenderness and said, "Take no for an answer. Her experiment is over." I could smell the deep soapy center of your still wet braid and stood there with panting nostrils. "If you're reasonable about it, and you get back to your own, unobjectionable little project, some other institution may accept you again somewhere, someday."

The scrambled egg bits were now assembled in a little mound in the center of my palm. My nails were white and clean again. I wanted to believe that someone would pardon me. I didn't think five years could shatter into glass shards. It'd be easy enough to complete my nearly complete thesis. But no matter what you're working on, there comes a time when you realize your work isn't worth doing. In my case, that time was Rachel's untimeliness.

I knew from the melody of the way you'd said "someday" that you had nothing more to say. I rose to find a trash can, you rose to dismiss me before I could leave, I left before I could find the trash.

I have always stood outside your office door for a long time after I close it. You must hear the pause between the latch and my steps. I stand at your door and your name plaque hits exactly eye level. JOAN in my left eye, then my invisible nose, then KALLAS in the right, in white block letters that are etched into fake wood and full of dust. Sometimes I clean a little dust out. Sometimes I blow. The portion of your life I estimate I take up on any given day has been the size of my pride. Hugely variable.

Your husband, unbuttoned to the nipples, stood chatting a sophomore when I got out onto the quad. I walked right up to them and flicked the eggs into the can beside the girl. I nodded to Barry but he didn't want to acknowledge me, lest he offend her. He curbs his natural mess via some kind of "one at a time" rationing I see his entire flesh struggling to uphold. Would he have acknowledged you? Of course. The sophomores know about you, Barry's better half, so much better. He'd be lessening himself to distance himself from you in any way. He does know that, to his credit.

"Why Mr. Estlin," I said, sticking a wooden spoon into his seduction, "what fine autumn weather. Unbutton your shirt once deeper and admit the entire breeze."

"Nell."

He thrust one chest hair and a low button into the wrong hole.

"I'm Catherine," said the sophomore. To my delight, she shook my hand.

I left him to his bad hobby. The campus is raw and at its neat best in September. I'm disgraced Joan but also outraged. Now that the shock is wearing down, I can begin to mourn that this bully of a Parthenon is no longer open to me. As I walked past the library, Tom went flying up its stairs. He didn't see me and I didn't call out to him, though it would have been a tonic to stare at the eternal and reliable mole on his neck. Your class tomorrow would have been the first we've seen of each other since our split. He doesn't know that I won't be there. He'll sit next to Mishti, your two blithe out-of-department guests, their host missing.

Home now, I open to aconite. The venom Cerberus spat at Hercules as the hero dragged the beast out of Hades. Wolf poison. A genus of nearly three hundred species of flowering plants, most grow in mountain meadows, most have the power to asphyxiate. I want to begin with the blue-flowering variety because it is the quickest to close the throat.

MONKSHOOD

TWO PRIESTS DIED IN DINGWALL IN 1856 WHEN THE COOK GRATED monkshood root into the evening stew, mistaking it for horse-radish. I've been gathering legends of Aconitum, monkshood's parent toxin, and they pop up everywhere. In Shasekishu, in Shakespeare, in Medea. In the funny little pamphlet on your windowsill from the British Homeopathic Association. Hapless thirteenth-century Japanese servants mistake dried aconite root for sugar and almost, but do not, die of it. Henry IV imagines the poison as blood mingled "with venom of suggestion." Medea fails to poison Theseus with aconite-tipped wine. Athena, armed with aconite, transforms Arachne into a spider. The moon goddess Hecate invents aconite one night in her garden. She wants it both for poisoning her enemies and for boiling into teas for teething or feverish children. She extracts it from the dirt, right at the spot where saliva dripped from the many mouths of Cerberus, hound of Hades, dragged by his leash out of hell and into the sunshine.

See Dracula: if the lady Mina will keep aconite in her bed-chamber, she will be safe from the vampire. Rudolph Bloom, father of Leopold, kills himself by an aconite overdose.

No plain antidote is yet known. I'm designing its antidote, or at least I'm designing a tiny botanical firefighter who can climb the poison's ladder and hose it down, put out the flames, save the cat. I need to cold-soak and freeze the monkshood seeds for three weeks before I can sow them. They're in the freezer right now. I'm building, if you'll help me, a new aconite that accepts its own opposite. Think of it as me and you alone together. A poison that undoes itself.

RACHEL

RACHEL HAD JOINED OUR LAB FROM THE METALS SIDE; I'D BEEN THE flower girl, and Jason the synthetics, alongside three others whose work I couldn't classify. We thought of ourselves as grungy, secular-age saviors who would eventually be able to detoxify toxins faster than ever before, the way microchips made computers smaller than ever before, and in doing so advance our society. Rachel worked on the binding of ferric hexacyanoferrate, picturesquely called Prussian blue, to thallium, its chemical enemy. Depending on hydration state and particle size, this binding could be praised with the name of *antidote* in its most successful cases. Rachel approached her venture with such American A+ confidence, such loony eagerness to do right, she turned away from thallium's essential danger and focused on its weakness. She believed it to be a fallible menace and believed herself to be an agent of immunity. The upper bound for skin exposure to univalent thallium ions is 0.1 milligram per square meter of skin in a forty-hour work week. Rachel's weekly hour totals exceeded eighty as a matter of pride.

When exposed to air, thallium becomes clear, tasteless, and odorless. I guess even the most stringent precaution can't protect against invisible attack. I wonder when it was that it reached her. Once inside the body's cells, thallium binds to sulfur, damages the 60S ribosomes, and fatally disrupts the functioning of our proteins. She may have touched it, inhaled it, ingested it. She wore splash goggles, gloves, and a dust respirator. She did know the bigness of the risk.

I didn't know her very well, as I've told you. I admired her so I left her alone. I liked the short hairs on the back of her neck. I liked how her cheeks collided with her goggles when she smiled. I liked that she neither wore deodorant nor shaved her armpits. That secret hair soaked up and spread a smell so rank I'll never unsmell it. I liked her adamance, her clarity, her wristwatch, and her gusto. I liked that she had been born. The loss is serious and I accept my piece of it. But what am I to do with the seeds in my freezer, this set of toxins unremedied, Rachel's project incomplete, and the prospect of disqualifying myself from your absolutely necessary nearness?

The university gave us an afternoon to empty our lab lockers. The only thing I kept in my lab locker was a stick of beef jerky that I'd bitten into over the summer and never finished. I chewed up that rock-hard half-jerky and then I stole Rachel's tinted goggles from their peg on the wall, and the two giant Zanzibar castor seeds that I had ordered for the lab, and the monkshood sample we hadn't collectively decided what to do with. These things were mine, by right, or at least I would best appreciate them.

I'd become sort of frantic thinking about the physical horror of what had happened to her. Frantic, and disgusted with myself and my humdrum studies and my whole pasty anemic priceless life. I couldn't find any way through it except to continue her project, as if that somehow preserved or resuscitated her person. But nobody else wanted to touch it, I suppose understandably so. I wanted to touch it. Not the thallium, that'd be dumb and redundant, but the other avenues, the castor, the monkshood, the other toxins we'd wanted to unwind and to heal. Rachel's focus hadn't been our only option, it had only been her only option. I knew that if we could quicken a detoxification starting with any other seed, set a speed record, she'd approve, she'd even celebrate, in some breathtaking, gravityless way that only dead dancers know about.

Sam and Adrian and Jason and Evelyn emptied their nicely stocked lockers into Columbia totes and big blue IKEA shopping bags—sweatshirts and workbooks and rainboots and Nalgenes—as if this were merely a domestic disturbance, as if it were merely time to move out. They didn't fuss, or fight, or reject the event in any way. Jason's already been given another post in the textile fibers study. Evelyn can only function if she is doing what she's told—she seemed to love being told to leave, it was such an easy instruction to execute. She rolled up her Science Under the Stars T-shirt so neatly it fit *inside* her Nalgene, and then she thunked the Nalgene into the shaft of her rubber boot. The way these things fit together seemed to hypnotize her into deep relief. Sam and Adrian were high when they came in, and in retrospect I realized they had often been high. They didn't see or care about the beans and the seeds. I looked around the room. These were the only other four humans who knew the beans and the seeds existed, they were leaving two-by-two like the schoolgirls in *Madeline*, and then the lab would be professionally cleaned out and zeroed, a half hour after we left.

I guess you could say that I like revenge and they like common decency. I guess you could say I don't approve of myself enough to protect myself. I guess you could say to each their own. The biggest difference between us is that nobody else in our lab had you to lose—you, too botanical for metals or synthetics, you, flowers-only.

They studied by the light of their own Joans, no doubt, but I live by you.

Your class continues this semester, indifferent to my absence, as if I weren't its blood, pumping minerals and force from the second row. Admit that I make you possible. Admit, at least, that you make me possible. So much you already know. Tom and Mishti are taking your class because I told them to. Because they thought we would take it together. They now get to sit in whichever row they pick, in your presence, in your presence that suffers in its luster from the lack of me, because some destinies are kind and some are pickled.

KANSAS

WHEN YOU GROW UP IN KANSAS WEARING VERY LARGE SHORTS, thinking not very much of yourself, thinking mainly of your knees, looking mainly at your knees, your face a frisbee that can't fly, your teeth buck, your eyebrows rectangles, your forehead more than half of your face, your shirts shapeless, your shape shapeless, your Kansas shapeless, your lust absent, your legs bowed, your arches flat, your chest flat, your ears your only curves, your ears never pierced, your denim never dazzled, your sneakers white, your socks white, your teeth turquoise with rubber bands, your cheese orange, your milk whole, your bread wonder, your luxury a tuna casserole, your pale a neon pale, your fantasy to race a Mario Kart over the desert and into the final oasis, your earthly oasis a salted pretzel, your solitude total, your urges not even visible to you on the clearest days at the farthest horizons, your blank magnificent, your inertia wild and authentic, your nothing your preference, and then into it somebody walks, a Joan, this sudden hero can really take control.

You're susceptible first to idolatry, then to study, to apprenticeship, and finally to a kind of patient love that makes fun of itself and believes in itself without limit. Imagine being a pudding cup of a person and encountering a confident, elegant, powerful scholar who knows what to do with her shoulders. Imagine encountering you.

You don't wear any kind of coat until the first snow of the year.

You eat milk chocolate for breakfast and canned pineapple for lunch and sweet potatoes for dinner. You are a very ambitious ice skater. You can count to twenty in four languages and say "God Save the Queen" in Hungarian. You considered joining the Russian Orthodox Church after learning that the ballerino Nureyev was born on a Trans-Siberian train. You ask your students to read Kafka's diary entry about the Apple Seller before the semester begins to show that administration is everywhere *and* genius is possible. You celebrate Flag Day. You're afraid of turtles. You don't know that I know you're afraid of turtles. You climbed the Matterhorn. You can drain the insides of an egg through a pinhole. You paint perennial vines onto drained eggs. You watch *The Godfather Part II* when you're sick. You scrub your shower grout. You get your students good jobs and give them terrible grades. You love your dog. Once upon a time you loved your mother.

It's acceptable to admire you. Admiration is the natural starting point and I did start there. Admiration is love without expectation and I'd be psychotic to expect. It was only when you told me to admire myself—that I was capable, that you noticed me, that I stood out, that I deserved, who knows what I deserved—that I began to imagine myself as an adult human with arms and legs. I began wearing pants that fit me around the waist. I began wearing long-sleeved shirts when it was cold outside as opposed to several stacked short-sleeved Hanes undershirts. I began to brush my teeth at night *and* in the morning. I began to hold myself responsible for myself, so that I could hold myself accountable to you. So that you wouldn't change your mind about me.

You never minded all that much, altogether. It's always been such a lukewarm encouragement between us—you are essential to me and I am okay to you—but lukewarm is about as hot as I get. What thrilled me about you was your absolute needlessness. You didn't seem to need anybody's approval, friendship, witness, or opinion. You didn't need color, flavor, vacation, or exercise. There was this crystalline and atomic permanence in your center that I knew you'd inherited from some original lord. It made me feel that if I worked very hard, I could be as alone and as perfect as whatever that thing is inside you. You made me feel irrelevant and totally free.

Freedom can be hard to come by when you grow up in land-locked Kansas, located exactly at the midpoint between the Pacific and Atlantic oceans, which means you have the farthest way to go either way to get out, which means you must get out, eventually, after you grow out of Kansas, which you didn't, which I did, which is the first plain fact about me, the place I will perpetually be in the process of exiting, just as you are the far and temperate and coastal state I am always and never entering.

MISHTI

MISHTI SINGH WORE TEN NECKLACES TO YOUR CLASS AND I HEAR you didn't like them. What you need to understand about Mishti is that she doesn't wear necklaces because she's making an effort, she wears necklaces because her neck deserves them. Her complete beauty is demanding and it's an act of respect on both her and our parts to oblige it. Think of Mishti as *full*. This is the perfect opposite of your austerity and I find the thought of you standing near each other entertaining. Mishti grew into not only the common assets of a full chest and hips, but full brows and full eyelids, full muscular shoulders, full mustache hair she waxes bimonthly.

I saw the ruby leotard she wore, tucked into an ankle-length skirt that showcased her plummy ankles. Mishti does things to improve herself and believes that she can be improved. The little galaxy she releases herself into repeatedly assures her that she is not only improved but ideal. You'll confuse her if you scoff at her. Besides, she'll execute your work immaculately and you will never find a solitary point to deduct.

Mishti grew up in Jackson Heights, Queens, the middle child of many, daughter of a chemist and a doorman. Her mother is named Anjali, she is the Senior Protein Expression and Analytics scientist for Pfizer East Coast. Her father is named Gopi, he is the early morning shift doorman at 60 West 13th Street and his name means "protector of cows." Her siblings are all academically accomplished and aesthetically darling, and she's differentiated herself via this galactic style. Personally I cheer for her. I hope you'll eventually join me, because until you do, I'm going to hear about it.

She came over to my place after your class to talk about Tom. It became, of course, a conversation about the death and the verdict and the degree and only much later about the breakup. This makes it sound like there are things going on in my life when in fact there is nothing. But Mishti (whose name means "sweet person") has been in Cincinnati all summer, interning for Procter & Gamble. I hadn't bothered to catch her up because I haven't, as a matter of principle, been bothering.

I told her I had stolen the beans and the seeds. She told me I'd lost my mind. I told her that for the first time in my long drab studies I had some new and exciting work to do, Rachel's work. She asked if castor and monkshood were as deathly as thallium. I told her no, not as deathly, mostly scary if swallowed. She asked if I thought I'd be able to bring them back to a different lab. I told her it's hard to sell a stolen painting. She asked how my parents had taken it and I said I hadn't told them. My parents are retired now and I try, as I said, not to bother them. Mishti finds this puzzling because she's better friends with her parents than with her friends. Her mother *has fun* within herself and manages to bring Mishti in on it. The Anjali Singh of Mishti's childhood came home from the lab and started whistling, flinging her shoes around, frying things, pummeling the cat, encouraging all her children to crawl under the kitchen table and see what they could find down there.

My parents, to their credit, built a fun of their own, one to which I have never been openly invited. Their bi-religious marriage provoked such loathing from both sides, I think they coped by building a code, a secret language of defiance that I could hear them speaking to each other, and admire, but never really learn, having nothing of my own to fight against, having not earned the badge necessary to enter their rebels' club. I don't know whether getting expelled counts as a badge. I didn't risk anything, I only lost everything. Loss doesn't earn you any kind of dollar.

It was only after we'd talked about Tom and how distressed he'd looked in class and how he'd refused to tell her anything that she admitted you hadn't liked her necklaces.

"How do you know?" I asked.

"She pursed her lips at me."

"Joan's lips are naturally pursed."

(You can roll your eyes here without missing the next line.)

"No, but, she *looked* at my necklaces, and *then* she pursed."

"Joan rejects embellishment."

"What about her braid?"

"Her braid is her weapon."

"And the earrings?"

"I don't know, I've come to think of them as her ears."

"They're big hunks of stone."

"Embellishment for the severe."

"A severe celebrity botanist? I want her to like me."

"I've been trying for five years."

"She's, like, your best friend."

"From your lips to her ears."

I looked just then at Mishti's lips. There was a total and profound sculptural rightness to her face she had neither elected nor destroyed. I felt the honor of participating in the brief, biological fact of this sweet person's tiring existence.

"Do the work," I said to us both, "Joan's only in it for the work."

"In what?"

Mishti ran off with a clang of her bangles to meet Carlo at Hungarian Pastry. I knew it would take her over an hour on the F to the A B C to get from Smith-9th up to 110th and I didn't think the B was running. It was absurdly inconvenient that I had moved down here, she hollered, halfway down the stairs. Then, from the bottom, "You've got mail." I skipped down after her, forgetting the unscrewed screws that cover the steps and taking a nice deep poke in the foot. There it lay, half under the door and laughing at me, my last check from the registrar's office. It felt like setting an egg. I'd deposit it, then boil myself until the timer beeped zero.

CARLO

CARLO PARADA BURST INTO OUR LIVES AS IF ON HORSEBACK, ONE Sunday night, his jaw straighter and firmer than the line at a base of a triangle. If beauty loves beauty, he and Mishti could not have avoided each other for long. Back in April, when the Callery pears had flowered and Mishti had decked herself in blushes and golds, we walked past this guy crossing 117th. He stopped, turned, and followed Mishti's scent back to its source. There she was, only half a block farther up Broadway. He overtook us and then cut across me, stopping and facing us. It seemed he was our combined height.

He extended a hand to Mishti and said, "You're incredible."

"I'm Mishti," she actually replied. I kicked her calf to express my disappointment. I found him as sexual as an Amtrak train. They shook hands. At that point I might as well have lifted her onto my shoulders so that she could see him better. She began rolling up her sleeves, which had fallen loose and now gave her an excuse to reveal her twig-wide jeweled wrists. I wondered what more she would do with her hands now that they had been prepared. She rested one on each hip, assuming what the life coaches call a "a power position." And to the extent that his sturdy architecture permitted it, he wilted.

Throughout the courtship month that followed, I'd get intermittent sexual progress updates, biographical data points, fresh letdowns, triumphant reassurances. His second year of business school would soon end and he was preparing for a career in General Affluence.

"You know the path," Mishti rattled, mouth full of wonderful mushrooms at Sal and Carmine's. "Texas, Harvard, Blackstone, the obligatory two years of hard labor at SAC, checking all the boxes, but he didn't get along with Steve."

"Who's Steve."

"Never ask him who Steve is."

"Shan't."

"Now he's got to figure out somewhere else to go because they're not going to hire him."

"And yet he looks with confidence into his future, knowing he will land where he lands, cat-footed."

"Basically."

I can eat about four times as much pizza as Mishti can.

She leaned back defeated by her one stupid slice and wiped all the grease off her chin. "But," and then I got the full story: how it all began in Galicia, how his parents had bravely but reluctantly moved from Spain to Argentina, where his father would direct the Banco Galicia of Buenos Aires.

"Then what?"

"Then they didn't like it."

So from South America to the American South, where Texas startled them with its everything. They'd tried Houston, seat of the Argentinian consulate, only to find it oppressively uncivilized, and landed in Austin, which meant a demotion for Carlo's father but an integrated, respectable high school for Carlo. Mishti thinks this nonprivileged public education tempered Carlo's international flair but I think it only confirmed his superiority. He was *better* than the

American boys. He could do more: he knew how to waltz, he knew how to surf, he knew how to shake someone's hand with a frankness uncurbed by American puritanism. The Austin taco culture had chilled him partly out, but it had also accentuated his elegance, the way salt releases the flavor in ice cream.

Carlo, like Tom, like myself, is an only child. The secretly nervous, lonely, son-of-a-workaholic-father and therefore fatherless boy at his core wears on me sometimes. From the way Mishti describes his youth, his after-school hours, he relied on his mother's affection so entirely—I worry about what Mishti will have to be for him in order to supply his steam. She doesn't seem to worry. Mishti is impossible to deplete. But I think you know what I have in mind. I have in mind a man whose pumpkin head and uncombed clown tufts lie as far from Carlo's majesty as the spectrum will allow, but who needs just as much, and who is sucking your life out as if through straws up each of your ear canals.

BARRY

ASSOCIATE DIRECTOR BARRY ESTLIN SERVES THE FIRST YEAR AREA of the Columbia Undergraduate Residence Halls and it is his *job* to be on good terms with the students. It is his job! He supervises not only Carman Hall but Furnald Hall, John Jay Hall, and even Hartley and Wallach Halls; he specializes in polishing the gem he calls *personal-academic balance*; he is a four-time winner of the Students Choose Award. For this, and I can't say what else, he gets to be married to you.

My favorite thing about Barry is his mother, whom I've never met, but whom I hear is Ohio's uncontested star dog-whisperer. Mrs. Ronald Estlin, Nancy to her friends, receives and boards dogs from across the 220-mile-wide state, the only admission requirement being that the dog has displayed signs of psychic unrest. Did you know that the state of Ohio is 220 miles long and the same 220 miles wide at its most distant points? And yet it isn't a square? Do you ever feel like the state of Ohio, an inherently even form of equal measures that has been twisted into something new, asymmetrical, and weirdly pointy? I don't think of you as weirdly pointy I'm just asking how you think of yourself. You know how I think of you.

Oh, Joan, I understand that Barry can be explained as Midwestern. And I so admire the work his mother does. Carrie, who heard it from Anna, who heard it from Jill, told me that Barry has told all three of them that his mother once cured a dog of its diabetes by blowing onto its eyeballs. Have you ever met this Mrs. Ronald? (Have you ever met Carrie, or Anna, or Jill?) I never ask about your participation in Estlin family holidays because I never ask, but if you and she have become close these past ten years a great portion of my woe would be softened. Nobody ever talks about Barry's father because there's something boring and a little embarrassing about how rich he is.

You married Barry when you were younger, braver, lonelier, poorer, and more frightened than you are now. You don't want a public divorce to interrupt your book sales, but now your book sales make Barry unnecessary—in a new way, a new way that completes the many old ways he has always been unnecessary, a new and undeniable way that demands action. You are quick to anger and slow to action.

I imagine Barry as a boy surrounded by drooling retrievers and long-haired wiener-poodles. I imagine a wiener-poodle as a miniature cross between a limousine and a sheep. I know, I know the dogs did Barry good. I know they are responsible for whatever care he exhibits that is untainted by incompetence, vanity, and lust. I wonder what his responsibilities were toward them: whether he was in charge of feeding or walking, poop-bagging or nighttime snuggles, and whether he carries out the same chores for your dog Amanda.

Tom's mother didn't allow dogs in the snow globe but here in Red Hook the going assumption is that all tenants are dogs themselves so please send Amanda my way whenever she's in need of a field trip. She is welcome here. I don't yet (and won't ever) have any furniture, rugs, or human food in the house for her to damage or ingest. Meanwhile there are very large windows through which she can see clouds of every shape, some of which might remind her of herself. I think she'll really like it here and I promise not to test my late-blooming monkshood blossoms on her. I wouldn't test my late-blooming monkshood blossoms on anybody except myself.

The more I settle into my private exile, the more I realize what it means to be seen. The biggest difference between you and Barry is that while you both need to be seen, you, once seen, are quelled, whereas Barry, once seen, sees back. He acts upon the seer. He wants to be seen again. He never wants the seeing to end. He believes he has an infinite amount to reveal, a body full of secrets to hand out as rewards to the loyal witness. The single most dangerous thing about Barry is he spends his days getting thanked—thanked for his guidance, for his attention, for his good vibes—a tradition that has instilled in him both a knee-jerk humility and a much deeper belief in his own indispensability.

The architect who dispensed with him in the nineties, what was her name, something very nice, Rhonda, Rhonda Davies, she did him real damage and, in flinging him your way, damaged you too (and with you obviously me). Here's what I've gathered about Rhonda, based on Image Search: Rhonda had a head of gray hair at age twenty-five. The day the last black strand left her head she went out and bought a wardrobe's worth of Eileen Fisher. She draped shawls over her premature age and anointed it with power, signified dignity, became a magnet for dignity-addicts. She was a woman who derived power from the way people treated her, rather than from any inner force. She mesmerized Barry until she bored him. Barry entertained her until he disgusted her. And then there you were: slight Joan, in your tight black clothes, the opposite of

Rhonda's loose beiges, Joan, altogether dark, who took up no space in a room and radiated inner force.

I will never blame Barry for falling in love with you but I will blame him for considering himself eligible. He is listed as the Decapitated Chaperone for The Halloween Hoedown next month and most of my ex-section students from Elements to Organisms are going. Jill and Carrie have cut two face holes into a large Casper mattress delivery box and are going as a Twix bar. My first thought is: the box will block Barry's view. My second thought is total despair. What if they'd gone as kittens, or themselves, or anything not wrapped in cardboard? Barry might have spontaneously combusted on them. And called it the costume's fault.

Anybody should punch anybody in the face with beauty, at any time, without getting punched back by a penis. I want Carrie to be as unbearably saturated in herself as she is, and then to fear no retribution from the less saturated. To thank Associate Director Barry Estlin for his advice about the laundry services in Furnald Hall and to leave that conversation knowing the conversation has ended.

You'll use the word *harmless*. I'll get back to my work.

CASTOR

THE CASTOR BEAN PLANT IS GETTING CLOSER BECAUSE ONE SEED will kill you but its oil will soften your stool. That's the kind of harm-unharm pairing I want. Imagine if I could coat a seed in its own oil, such that right before you die you expel the entire contents of your bowels, emptying yourself wholesale, actually emancipating yourself. Imagine how light and speedy you'd feel in the afterlife. And how hungry. You'd spend eternity ready for lunch and your family would develop a mortal dread of diarrhea, a symptom of their grief that would last the rest of their lives, until they too took the oil-coated bean. Finally you'd all be light and speedy, all together.

Ricin, the parent toxin, needs to be expelled quickly or not fully metabolized. If you swallowed the bean without chewing, for instance, you'd probably make it. Or if you chewed and I pumped your stomach within two hours. If you don't die in three to five days, you live. Even inside the bean itself there's a good cop bad cop: the ricin protein is a strong cytotoxin but a weak hemagglutinin, and the Ricinus toxin (also in there) is a weak cytotoxin and a strong hemagglutinin. The Ricinus can't penetrate your intestinal wall, but the ricin can. It seems everything wants to be very near to its opposite. I picture Ricin and Ricinus as twins, as Romulus and Remus, Romulus who will eventually kill Remus but who for now lies beside him, cozy and sucking from the teats of a she-wolf. That's the way to prosper, spooning someone who represents a total otherness. What a relief. Every morning you skip the mirror and look instead right into the eyes of your perfect antithesis. Then, thank you so much, some breakfast.

Ricin is six thousand times more poisonous than cyanide and twelve thousand times more than rattlesnake venom. The seeds look like small round zebras and the flowers look like Elmo's head and they're the most deadly seed on earth. You wouldn't believe how attractive the whole plant can be, forty feet tall and its leaves star shaped. Let us pity the Bulgarian communist defector (can you believe his name was as cute as Georgi) who got murdered by a ricin-tipped umbrella. He was just waiting for a bus on Waterloo Bridge. He didn't get any of the pleasure of the striped seeds, the fluffy flowers, the poison went via pellet right into the back of his thigh (the guy with the umbrella-gun said "Sorry" before running away) and Georgi thought nothing of it until he lay in the hospital dying.

The plant's family name is sardonically Euphorbia. The "b" snuck in as a hidden warning. I've stroked castor plants in the Brooklyn and New York Botanical Gardens, in the Conservatory Garden on 105th Street, in the Bronx Zoo. The bean can be detoxified by boiling, but that's like disqualifying the toxin in advance. If you're in the disqualifying game for, say, farming reasons, squeezing the boiled seed releases the oil, and the remaining hulls can be used in pressed-cake form for animal feed (sheep can withstand 10 percent castor bean meal in their rations without any ill effect). In humans, the detoxified bean can be used against leprosy, syphilis, boils, carbuncles and bunions and corns, warts, inflammation of the middle ear, toenail fungus, cysts. Castor oil in the eyes soothes membranes irritated by dust. Women in countries more imaginative than our own have traditionally lined the inside of the vagina with castor oil for birth control. But what about a woman who eats the whole bean, unboiled, and then needs to be saved? How do we boil the bean inside her?

The lab's two giant Zanzibar castor seeds look like the fanciest ladybugs, I love them, and I'm planting them tonight.

TOM

MAY TOM OTTAWAY NEVER PENETRATE ME AGAIN BUT I REST A LIFE-long heartfelt appreciation upon his head, his gentle head, a head I genuinely adore.

"Well Nell," he said as I climbed up out of the 1 train, his first peace offering since our breakup, a rhyme he's always disproportionately enjoyed. Maybe he wants me to call him "Tom Bomb," or "Don Tom," but he's too mild and spiritually castrated for either. "My condolences," he said.

"Tom," I said.

He sighed unemotionally. I am too mortified to accept condolences, sympathy, or awareness of any kind. We started walking.

If I am cold to Tom it's because heat sources molest him. He walks up the street between random admirers as if through a colonnade of lawn sprinklers, each wetting him from the side. He never returns the eye contact but I know he is soothed by the steady, quiet praise. These strangers leave him free to keep on, and in asking nothing of him, they really give him what he needs. I was one rare and temporary returnee of eye contact and I lasted two years, the longest ever detour on Tom's path toward individual fulfillment.

We met in the library where he used to sit on Tuesdays and Thursdays, rubbing his own scalp while he bent over art books too large to carry home. He was getting a master's in Medieval and Renaissance Studies, a course of study that was expensive and useless for him but deeply felt. I liked to do my cell biology homework at his table because when I got bored I could look at his hair, which seemed to me not to be possible. It was long as Samson's and never tangled and it covered his shoulders like a prayer shawl. Eventually he also got bored and we started talking—there was no one else at the table. After only a few dry kisses he learned that I lived with Mishti in a rat-friendly studio on Avenue C and he invited me to squat at Veronica's (the way he referred to his childhood home). I did this because I did this. Every night Tom and I would sleep in a bed that was too large for any child and too small for a pair of grown-ups.

The word I first associate with Tom's body is *utopia.* He's got the ridiculous ringleted black curls and a face cut from marble and flooded by moonlight. His body is long and smooth and consists entirely of untoned muscle. Nothing about him (except maybe the hair, his body is lovely but bland) distracts from the basic completeness and symmetry of his eyes, which have no discernible pigment and are a winter cloud gray. He and Mishti could repopulate the world perfectly; my two best friends have our species' two best faces. You could hardly call my face a face, more a perfunctory set of features that get the job, as it were, done. I approved of Tom without needing to be approved of in return. He found this relaxing.

All of the love Tom has ever received in his life has come to him unearned, so to ask him to start earning it now would be like charging to use the bathroom. We maintained a totally successful, fraternal, mutual regard. I was surprised by his ability to be so beautiful and he was equally surprised by my ability to define *ribosome* and there we left it, a kind of handshake of the wills, and we sat contented there, beside each other, for two years, until we more or less simultaneously smelled the pungent decay of our own inner yearnings.

We're friends now, which is most of what we ever were. Tom refers to the relationship as "A Disappointment in Love." He's heavy into tapestries and goblets, for context. We walked across the park toward his mother's snow globe to pick up my personal effects. I knew we'd be alone there; Veronica spent Mondays in Litchfield. I didn't want to be alone with Tom anymore but I was capable of it, it was something I would always know how to do. We were both wearing new jackets but the same shoes we had worn during our relationship. Looking down as we walked up the bike path, it could almost have been one of the 716 days we'd spent in our Disappointment.

Tony the doorman welcomed us both as we entered. It occurred to me that he didn't know about the breakup and neither of us bothered to tell him. We proceeded by habit to the elevator. Frankie the elevator man yanked the grate open for us. Frankie didn't know either and I told him immediately.

"Won't be seeing you anymore, Franks."

He shut the grate and the elevator lurched into service.

"You two done boinking?"

"Never to boink again."

"Shame."

"Shame."

"Shame," Tom chimed in, generously.

The eleventh floor dinged and we stepped from the elevator into the apartment, which was in itself the building's eleventh floor. Tom's grandfather had been a British gentleman; Tom's father had been a gentleman's renegade son. Grandfather Ottaway had removed the family stain Junior to this owned asset on Madison, a few blocks from the Metropolitan Museum. Junior met Veronica on the steps of that museum, married her, missed Tom's birth at McCloskey's Bar, and died shortly thereafter of liver disease. Tom doesn't drink for this reason and lives instead in the self-intoxicated state of medieval unicorn daydreaming, his substitute vice.

Thomas Ottaway the Third now flipped on the light switch in his bedroom and stretched out over a window-side chaise lounge. There lay an infinite waywardness about him, a quality many found unforgivable in one whose *way* had been so neatly paved by such lavish means, but which was as natural and inherent to him as the means were, and which he could no more separate himself from than from his surname. Finding the chaise lounge hard, he got up again. He walked through the snow globe as if through a school: cowed, quiet, easy. I walked through it in an aggressively neutral state I'd adopted for coping with riches that would never improve my life.

His mother's framed face reigned over the piano. Veronica had always been intelligent and silent and given Tom very little instruction, reprimand, or fawning. Tom had been her young business partner in the business of being alive rather than dead, and she had treated him rather as a colleague. She'd worked as a Corporate Patron Program officer for the Met's Development Office since the eighties and when Junior died she remarried the curator of Northern European and British Painting, a very short man named Harvey. Harvey had been on the brink of proposing himself when Junior beat him to it—he'd warned Veronica right then that the man was a drunk—and Harvey hadn't been waiting for Junior's death *per se* but for the inevitable day when he would die. Junior having obliged him entirely, Harvey married Veronica within eight months.

The new family stayed in the city until Tom had finished fifth grade at Dalton and could be sent to a loosely Christian boys' boarding school, a context in which Tom was at all times two notches too feminine and where he would spend seven years. Tom can still fit into his eighth-grade basketball shorts. Harvey and Veronica progressed from spending weekends to weekdays to the entirety of their recent retirement in Litchfield, Connecticut, leaving the gaping snow globe to Tom in all his slightness. A new distillery in Litchfield ages and bottles coffee-flavored bourbon. Harvey invites Tom to come up and enjoy the guided corn and barley boiler tour about once a month, an act of decorum so ignorant of Tom's personality that it could be taken as insult but which in practice is ideal because neither party needs to fear any actual contact.

I could feel Tom's boredom radiating from his elbows and knees. He lacked an active companion. Women shrink from forcing uninvited intimacy on him, partly because he never invites it, and partly because they mistake his beauty for its frequent synonym pride, but pride in Tom is only a mellow bashfulness. He is doing most of the shrinking himself. Shrinking from his guilty and morbid inheritance, from his nice face he can't undo, and from his inability to understand anything about himself other than his inheritance and his face. I feel for Tom because he's trying, like anyone, to figure it out.

When he found a more comfortable place to lie down on his mother's bed, I began gathering my things. I'd left a water-flossing gun in the middle bathroom, a sweater under his bedside table, and six bags of Pirate's Booty in a kitchen cupboard because the Ottaways don't believe in snacking. I'd already Ubered my suitcase and bookcase to Red Hook and I was surprised to realize there wasn't anything else of mine anywhere. Mishti still has my colander. I guess I haven't really *lived* anywhere in a long time, maybe since Kansas.

He was still on his mother's bed when I returned. Seeing him there, spread out over the poppy and marigold duvet, I had a Pavlovian instinct to give him head. It would have been easy, these were the khakis I knew well with the two little buttons, and beneath them his absolutely fine dick, a dick I would have been happy to babysit, or feed, forever, as if it were a well-behaved cat.

"Joan is rather something," Tom said just then, terrifying me because I couldn't tell how he'd connected the dots between his dick and you, a dot path I've traced countless times.

I bought myself about forty seconds of recovery time by going to get my backpack from his room. When I came back, he'd sat up on the bed and I began packing the floss gun and its various wires.

"How would you feel if I described you as *rather something*?" I said instead of saying anything.

"How could you? It's exactly what I'm not."

"So it's a compliment?"

"She's magnificent."

"How would you feel if I described you as *magnificent*?"

"How could you not? It's exactly what I am."

"You think Joan sees you that way?"

"Can Joan see? Sometimes I think she and Homer exist in trans-time mutual blindness where they can only see each other and no other idiots."

I felt a little nauseated because I could tell he was going to know you very well.

"She even hates Mishti, number one non-idiot."

"I heard. Mishti has never been hated before."

"I haven't either," Tom said, as if asking himself whether that could be true.

"I hate you," I said reassuringly.

"Ah," he said, reassured.

"You're not even in Joan's department, she's hosting you—"

"What do you care? I need a little botany for the Netherlandish analysis."

"I'm saying you're her guest, you're not even doing the problem sets, you're a pain in her side, so leave her alone"—did he know I was begging?—"attention makes her angry and you aren't her type."

"Hey, have you seen Mishti's new type?" He was suddenly jolly.

"The Earl of Argentina?"

"A specimen!" Tom made himself snort. I admired the way Tom admired other paragons with such innocent and unenvious glee. "He gives me goosebumps."

"But what does he give Mishti?"

"Also goosebumps."

The floss gun, sweater, and snacks filled my backpack to the drawstrings. I tightened them and buckled the top. I was, rather cleanly, ready to leave the snow globe.

"I'm going to make Joan like me," he declared, staring into the eyes of a porcelain basset hound that lay mournfully across his mother's mantel. "People like me, that's all I've ever had."

"And you had a great girlfriend, for a while."

"But I don't anymore, and you don't even go to this school anymore either, which is fine, because you monopolized Joan anyway. Rest in peace, Rachel Simons."

"Make Mishti like you."

"I'm a lost cause with Mishti—look at me, I can't even multiply fractions. Carlo can do the spreadsheets."

"The spreadsheets? What do you know about Carlo's spreadsheets?"

"He came to pick her up from class yesterday and he was, like, holding them."

"Holding spreadsheets?"

"Joan just missed him but I bet she would have found him, if not her, rather impressive."

"Stop saying *rather*. You're all hanging out now?"

"You could have tackled Rachel, peed on her thallium, and thwarted this woeful destiny—"

I thanked Tom for letting me get my things and buzzed the call bell for Frankie. I could always rely on Frankie to receive my distress signals and the light starting rising at once from L through 2 3 4. I watched the numbers light up and go dark. Tom hadn't bothered to walk me out and he hollered something from Veronica's room I couldn't hear—I caught the word *old*. The 10 glowed and faded. My guardian cherub peeled back the rusting grate and welcomed me into his chariot.

OAKS

THE PARK FELT WEIRDLY EXTRA WIDE THAT AFTERNOON AND WHO knew a water flosser could be so heavy but I came to see you right away because hearing your name in Tom's mouth had totaled me.

You were locking up your office. I took your keys out of your hand and walked in. I don't know why I wanted to start with you mad.

"I have somewhere to be."

"I don't!"

"Nell why don't you do something, work on something again—your original note on phylogenesis was inane enough I could have sent it to Bioinformatics. I guess I could still send it to Bioinformatics."

"Trees are boring."

"If you publish something now, you stand a chance at reapplying somewhere else. Barry won't have ruined you completely."

You forced me to say the name, "Barry?"

"Well, no, not just Barry. That would have been uncomfortable. Barry and the whole committee. Mendelson. Thompson. Peterson. The club of sons. They've made your life difficult, but how couldn't they? At least you hung on to your life."

I replayed their whale tones, their groaning, *Be-gone*. I hadn't been able to see through my helmet visor. I hadn't recognized Barry among the sons. I hadn't seen this particular facet of his previously incomprehensible power. It didn't seem plausible, it didn't even seem possible that a rational institution would assign him such a consequential appointment. "Barry is on the disciplinary committee?"

"Not just the disciplinary committee. He's on the higher boards. Several of them. The Estlins created this campus—they'll always control it. He's the current crown prince. Why do you think people love him?"

"Why do you love him?"

"Are you my therapist?"

"Are you still my adviser?"

"Expelled students don't have advisers."

"Are you?"

"Do something. Then I'll decide."

"I'm doing, I'm doing, but it's super scary stuff that could kill me so I'd like a little supervision."

"Oak trees are safe."

You rolled up your window shade, even though you were leaving the office and had somewhere to be, only to remind me how safe trees are. I saw you, for the first time, not as your individual self but as an accessory to the throne. I knew you would one day ascend to full power and that I would one day be hanged.

"Thank you for advising an expelled student who scares herself," I said robotically even though it was the deepest feeling in my body. I thought of Tom and Mishti, loyal subjects whom Barry had spared. "I hear you love all of my friends."

"You have friends?"

"I'm salty and plain so the pretty ones chew on me."

"Oh, Mishti."

"You think she's pretty!"

"She thinks she's pretty."

"She is. She does. And Tom."

"Who's Tom?"

"Ringlets."

"He couldn't bear to look up at me. He covered his face with his hair."

"I'd just broken up with him, he'll recover."

You looked a little alarmed and you moved Deren Eaton's book from your desk to a shelf for no reason. I took this as unbelievable flattery.

"I didn't realize you dated."

"I can have secrets."

"He has very nice hair."

"You have very nice hair."

The three snakes in your braid thanked me.

"Leave my office."

"Very well."

"Nell—" you said, almost kindly, as I turned your knob. "Get anything done."

I closed the door. Joan, my nose, Kallas. The line of your name looked like a horizon I'd approached, a threatening and unnatural arrival that meant I'd soon fall off the edge of the earth. I blew a little dust out from the lower curve of your J. I got that good and done.

BOOGERS

THESE DAYS WHAT I REALLY LIKE TO DO IS TO LIE ON THE FLOOR shirted and pantsless and relieve one or other nostril of a really good boog. I leave all boogers on the windowsill. In the morning I wipe them up. They look so different dry—less lovable, easier to discard. My little trash can is full of them. Mishti says *Nell is forgetting herself* but I say I've got world-class boogs.

Don't worry Joan I check myself. I check myself *and* I wreck myself. Sometimes I make tortellini and even if I make only half the bag, call it 1.5 portions, I pour it steaming into my bowl and I look at it and think: nobody in the whole world deserves this much tortellini. I love it so much, it doesn't need any topping, each tortellinus is a self-sufficient packet of perfect food. I love best the unforgivably dank tricolor frozen kind, manufactured by mass brands that put ammonium bicarbonate and cracker meal into the ricotta stuffing, tortellini that is probably unhygienic even while it is frozen. I can't believe I get to eat it.

Same trouble with a box of Kraft spirals and cheese. A whole box feels like the ideal portion size to my body but my mind knows it's supposed to feed five or whatever children and to hog it is unconscionable sin. It's okay, I use the empty box as one brick in my temple wall. I don't mean *my body as temple*, we know my body to be a rectangle with rounded corners, I mean the temple I am building to worship life.

One time in the cafeteria I heard you telling Barry to stop eating and even though Barry is fat and even though I understand your point and even though I have eaten as I've said more tortellini in my thirty-one years than any creature has ever merited in the history of the universe it was almost enough to cure me of loving you. Unfortunately, only almost.

I'm sorry I've become such a laziness, Joan. Your husband got me in big trouble and now I feel cosmically shy. But if I can just speed up this binding process by a minor increment we'll have made major progress and I'll redeem our rejected lab and Barry will have nothing on me and the many sons will turn back into little boys and Rachel will rest and we will all be able to suffer and heal and suffer and heal and suffer and heal whenever, whenever we need to. Neutrality will be our new pet drug.

UPAS

HARD TO SAY WHY THE MULBERRY'S CHINESE COUSIN WAS SUCH A huge hit with British nineteenth-century naturalists—the upas tree, their absolute staple nightmare. Joan what if every time Tom referred to you as "magnificent" I referred to you as "this ineradicable taint of sin, this boundless upas, this all-blasting tree"? That's Byron.

Jane Eyre tiptoed around "an upas-tree: that demon's vicinage."

Darwin's grandpa Erasmus dubbed it "the hydra-tree of death."

"She's a female upas tree," P. G. Wodehouse wrote about you. "It's not safe to come near her."

The problem with upas sap for my purposes is that it works too fast. No "Euphorbia" jokes here, the species Latin is straight *toxicaria*. The Chinese call it "Seven Up Eight Down Nine Death" because of how many steps you can take before it kills you: seven uphill, eight downhill, or nine on level ground. I'm not interested in that kind of immediacy. We need to stand a chance.

there stands an awesome Upas Tree
lone watchman of a lifeless land.

No bird flies near, no tiger creeps;
alone the whirlwind, wild and black

Pushkin. If a Russian thinks it's too bleak—the point is that I am the creeping tiger. I want in on the whirlwind. Let me in, tree, you were supposed to be safe. I can't believe you rolled up your window shade for me. That was a little sweetness in you, and they haven't installed an ID scanner in the Schermerhorn Extension. I'm going to come to your class.

PEDICULARIS

YOUR QUESTION: WHAT IS THE RELATIONSHIP BETWEEN POLLEN AND pistil in Pedicularis's floral evolution?

My question: What is the relationship between ricin and charcoal in a castor detoxification?

A genus of perennial green-root parasite plants. Broomrape family.

1983, Plitmann and Levin, Society for the Study of Evolution.

Plitmann working out of Jerusalem and Levin in Texas. "Different kinds of cowboys," your only joke of class. Everyone too nervous to giggle.

The activated charcoal mainly expels the ricin via vomiting. It's superficial that way, not a binding, just a purging. Rachel wouldn't be entirely satisfied. She'd fling grave mud at me. What kind of RIP is that.

"The multitude of floral architectures within angiosperms are complex adaptations (or adaptive strategies) insuring the transfer of pollen from a plant to another of the same species, the subsequent growth of the pollen tube in the style, and the fertilization of the ovule."

Nobody even giggled when Hans couldn't read "ovule" out loud.

Kugler, 1970; Frankel and Galun, 1977; Faegri and Van der Pijl, 1979; Cruden and Miller-Ward, 1981.

MAPLES

AFTER CLASS BARRY COULDN'T SEEM TO DECIDE WHICH IMPULSE was stronger: to touch Mishti's breast or to give Carlo one decisive fingernail scratch across the face that would mar him for a couple of months. He decided to make a comment about Mishti's molecular chemistry textbook.

"Molecular chemistry!" is what he came up with.

Carlo was wrapping Mishti's giant shawl around her and he had to make three laps before it stopped.

Barry is hugely excited that Mishti can do chemistry. I think it relieves him of an anxiety he houses about his own inability to do anything at all.

I stood holding this notebook in silence on the grass like a scarecrow.

"You're here?" Mishti said as if I'd brought her bad news.

"I've been hiding in the back."

Tom joined us. "Joan saw you."

"I thought Joan doesn't see."

"She saw you," he sulked, "I saw her see you."

"I'm Barry," Barry told Tom.

We were all standing in a circle and, if prompted, Barry would have hopped in the middle to dance.

"Carlo," Carlo shook Barry's hand.

Barry looked overwhelmed by so many members of his least favorite sex. He had presented himself to Tom and not to Carlo because Tom is as threatening as a wheat stalk. Carlo is as threatening as a six-foot-five dagger sheathed in velvet.

"I'm in the business school," Carlo went on, "and you're in Housing, is that right?"

I silently applauded his research and his insult.

"Director of the First Year Area."

Joan if you had been there would you have supplied the word *Associate*?

Carlo asked, "And the dean is Mendelson?"

My applause thinned and I started to hear Carlo's gears clicking. I couldn't guess why or how the MBA candidate had identified the undergraduate houser, even if his attitude suited me. I couldn't guess what he wanted with this Mendelson, who had apparently stood next to Barry and expelled me. There was no clear path leading from any of them to Carlo. Mishti had only come to your class twice. Your marriage to Barry is thankfully not widely reported. Carlo had only been dating Mishti a couple months. We were all essentially strangers. I thought of Carlo's spreadsheets, his format of choice, all the order and intention and menace that format contained.

"He is indeed," said Barry.

Tom: "Pun intended."

I had forgotten Tom was standing there, the wind had been blowing through him.

Mishti: "What are you talking about?"

Tom: "Sorry I thought he said *in-dean*."

Barry glowed. Mishti Singh had come to his defense.

"You're a clown," Mishti said to Tom, peeling Barry a grape.

Carlo said, "I love Mendelson." He brushed the pompadour off his forehead and focused. "He's going to fix Luxor's hiring freeze and open the whole thing up."

"Come by and meet him," Barry said, peeling Carlo a grape.

Carlo knew better than to say anything more. He'd gotten what he'd come for. His completely satisfied hair fell over his forehead again and stayed there, rustling a little when the wind blew. It was suddenly easy to picture him standing in the disciplinary committee horseshoe.

I looked to Tom for some familiarity, some family. His cloud eyes had narrowed and he'd been bothered. Mishti was looking at him too, still irritated. She was significantly enlarged and padded by her shawl and her little head emerged from it like a seal head from the sea. She'd recently cut her hair short, chin-length. The sharp edges of the front layers made her face look especially heart shaped.

Barry took over, now proud and comfortable. It was incredible to me that he could bear my company without guilt, but only compassionate people feel guilt. He asked Carlo, "What brings you to our side of campus?"

"My Mishti," Carlo said.

Mishti's soul purred under her padding. I became a silent and irretrievable turnip. Barry didn't want to process the fact of Mishti's unavailability so he turned to Tom.

"And you? I didn't catch your name."

"Thomas," Tom said, a thing I'd never heard him call himself.

"*Thomas*," echoed Mishti.

"I don't belong here either," Tom said, "but I'm trying to name the thistles in the seventh *Captivity* hanging and I thought maybe Joan could help me. Nell speaks very highly of Joan."

I'd never heard Tom say things like "speaks very highly" either and I wondered what kind of hat he was putting on.

"Me too," said Mishti, abstractly. "I wanted a break from Orgo and treated myself to some flowers."

And then you entered. It turned October yesterday and the campus maples are more than half red. Your hair is more than half gray. The midday sun did nothing to lighten the black of your sweater, your pants, your clogs. You saw us. You didn't really want to come near and you came just a little nearer. We are in the freshest part of autumn now. This was a pumpkin patch quality day. Your two stone earrings hung wearily from your ears and the left one got to nuzzle into your braid. I wished I could carve you a pumpkin.

Barry saw you and said, "My Joan."

Carlo smiled. Mishti smiled. Tom had his back to you and turned around, frantic. I wanted to remove the word *my* from Barry's vocabulary forever.

"Do I crash the Breakfast Club?"

Barry reached into his pocket and gave you an apricot. It was the most beautiful thing I'd ever seen him do.

Carlo wasted no time in saying, "Carlo." You shook his hand as if shaking hands with a bus stop. Carlo turned to Tom and said, "And I don't think we've met properly either, but, hey man." Tom smiled because he liked being called "man." Carlo put his arm around Mishti and turned her slightly, to announce that they would be leaving. Tom had nothing to say and seemed to want to have something to say. He kept smiling with his lips slightly parted. You must have sensed this and you told him, "Good eye with the bistort." Tom filled his hands with his own hair and threw it all over one shoulder, like he'd just won a sack of prize tomatoes.

I'm not going to fight Tom for you, I'm just going to rely on your better judgment.

Nobody asked you what a bistort is. Mishti just stood there and suffered. She'd done the problem set Tom hadn't done, and she'd worn her alpaca shawl. You didn't look at her once. You pushed a folder of problem sets into your large purse. Carlo and Mishti walked off. Tom was gone suddenly, the way Tom could sometimes suddenly go. Barry put his arm through your arm, as if he were your daughter.

"Behave yourself," you told me, peeling me a grape.

PYRAMIDS

"THEY COULD JUST RUN OFF TOGETHER," MISHTI LET ME IN, FUMING, "I don't care. Carlo's shoes are shiny *and* pointy maybe I got this whole thing wrong." We started up the stairs. "Maybe he just wants to run away with your ex-boyfriend. That would be cute, right? That would be cute."

"It's hard to say what you're talking about."

We paused on the landing between the second and third floors.

"Tom just stood there smiling at him!"

"We're talking about Tom?"

"About Tom's big crush on my boyfriend."

"Huh."

I had never considered how obviously almost gay Tom was, partly because it was so obvious; I figured Tom would have discovered it himself by now, if there was anything to discover. But it was certainly a likely and plausible option. Carlo seemed farther from it. We started climbing again.

"I think Tom was smiling because Carlo is a cool guy and Tom wants to be a cool guy too," I said from a few steps behind her.

"Well he's not going to become one by *smiling at them—*" Mishti's fury was convincing and unwarranted. "He should have punched Carlo in the shoulder."

"I guess I disagree."

We stopped at the fifth floor and panted quietly. She opened our old door.

"You want our menfolk to wage battle," I said. "Against each other."

"Yes. I want each to improve himself at the expense of the other. Then we will arrive at two evolved men."

I took my colander.

"I want Carlo to inspire Tom with loathing so great he leaps into action." She wasn't done. "Leaps! It doesn't matter where he lands." Now she was done.

I sat on the sofa and put eight of my fingers into the colander's holes. It was a nice one, coated in white ceramic, and the ceramic was cold, especially inside the holes. Mishti turned on the television. The screen filled with a paused DVD; I recognized Hrithik Roshan's face because he was her favorite. Mishti only watched Bollywood after three a.m. or in moments of high agitation. I loved to watch anytime. Hrithik was paused here in the middle of "You Are My Soniya," a musical number that required him to wear a black pleather bodysuit. We'd watched this dance the most times and it was some of the more successful male gyrating I'd encountered.

Mishti abruptly stripped and got in the shower. I liked the way she didn't need to watch the movie to feel its effects. I leaned back into the sofa. My fingers were cold now and I removed them from the holes and sat on them. The sweater I'd retrieved from the snow globe coughed up the smell of my past, every time I moved. I pulled the last Pirate's Booty from the bottom of my backpack.

The sad thing about this particular movie, *Kabhi Khushi Kabhie Gham*, is that the proud parents reject the poor bride and disown their son and exile the young couple into wretched misery. About six months ago I was very attached to this movie because it played out what would happen if Tom had married me. Veronica would have put on a ravishing sari and banished us to the Indian suburbs of London, far from our Delhi home, to start a new life without any family support.

I found it moving that the son missed the parents so much once in exile. My parents call me about twice a year; I may as well live in Southall. So far it hasn't hurt me, but this movie makes me wonder if I'm repressing myself.

The Booty was stale to the point of soggy but still almost erotically salty. I skipped the scene after "Soniya" and went straight to the next song, "Suraj Hua Maddham," a number that begins in an Indian street market and then moves to the sand between the Egyptian pyramids. In it, Veronica's son (he's too robust to be Tom, but he is an Indian Ottaway) wears an entirely translucent white blouse. He climbs to the top of the sand dunes and makes his body into the shape of a howling wolf against the setting sun. The subtitles say he is singing, "Why did the sky begin to melt?" His poor bride is wearing thick lines of kohl and looks perfect in her skirt, veil, and chestband—all red.

When they got to the part about "Oh, is this my very first love? My darling, is this my very first love?" Mishti started singing along from the shower. Her voice when she sings in Hindi is so gentle and high-pitched it has nothing at all to do with the very abrasive English speaker she also is. I liked Mishti's voice better than the poor bride's. After only a minute she came out with big drops running from her new short hair down her new naked neck and stood in her towel in the center of the living room, dripping.

"How did you really put up with him?" she asked. I paused the movie.

"Tom?"

"Didn't he just mope all over you all the time?"

"No."

"Didn't you wish he would wake up and do something?"

"Why is everyone always telling everyone to do something?"

You hate Mishti but you'd really like her.

"He could do something if he wanted something," she said.

"I think he does want something, he's just never needed anything, so it doesn't come naturally to him."

"What does he want? A unicorn of his own?"

The image of Tom's long black mane beside his unicorn's long white mane made me feel instantly and entirely relaxed.

"I think he wants to get a job."

"He doesn't know what jobs are."

"That's right."

Mishti reached the height of her frustration with Tom's elemental inefficiency and went back into the bathroom to get dressed. I pressed play.

"How beautiful this moment is!" They were singing. Mishti started singing again too. "Everything is changing! The dreams blend into reality." I read along and wished that I could sing. Mishti emerged in giraffe-print pajamas and sat next to me on the sofa. The disowned son sang, "Is this bond between us centuries old? Is that the reason why I'm meeting you like this?"

Is this bond between us centuries old? Is that the reason why I'm meeting you like this?

Suddenly they were in water. I couldn't tell if the water was near the pyramids or a new realm. His translucent blouse was now soaking wet translucent. The poor bride had changed into a turquoise sari that complemented the brown of the water mud. When she flung the veil back over her shoulder it smacked him in the face with a wall of spray and he looked as if he'd been waiting for that smack all his life. She kissed his Adam's apple. I'd never seen lip kissing in Bollywood so the neck kiss felt supremely sensual. Now they were dry again. Now *he* was in turquoise. Now she was translucent. A fourth realm welcomed them with its large globular rock formations. I wanted to move between climates this simply. I wanted to wear turquoise and collect every desert weed, herb, and bud. Finally, the street market again. Mishti turned it off.

"I can't tell you how much that movie means to me," I said sincerely, but I understand why she thinks I was joking.

"Leave me alone. Do you want to stay over?"

I'd fallen back into the feeling of things as they were when I lived there and Red Hook felt as far as Kansas. I said yes. Mishti pulled a full-size bed pillow out from under the couch and threw it at me. It knocked the colander off my lap. We laughed.

"You're probably right," I said, "Tom should do something. I should do something. You're the only one who ever does anything." Mishti knew and liked this about herself. She said nothing. Then she said, "Carlo does too."

I suppose one version of love is to match your nature with a similar nature. I can imagine that's pleasing because if you like yourself, you like your partner just as much. Personally I find Carlo stiff, but if Mishti admires him, that's more sustaining to her than coziness. Joan I could make you feel so cozy. My breath is always terrible but I will celebrate the innermost tenderness of you with a love you cannot picture and have never known before.

"What *are* you doing?" Mishti said. "Anything?"

"Don't turn this on me."

"I'm really asking."

"I don't know, Rachel would have set a new record for thallium binding if she'd, you know. I think—" Mishti's face settled into real listening. For the first time since I got expelled somebody was looking at me as if I were about to say something plausible. "I think I want to see how fast I can detoxify ricin, or maybe even aconite, whichever works first, make Columbia admit they gave up on us too fast, make Joan admit that I'm, or I don't know, make her, you know, *proud*, but first I have to grow them both from seed and without the lab's lamps and bases that's probably impossible." I didn't want her to stop looking at me. I said, "I don't know if that counts as doing anything."

She said, "Carlo's taking me to Bermuda for Christmas."

I pushed the pillow into the corner of the sofa arm and lay my head deep into it. Mishti stood up, turned off the lights, and went to bed, as if she were going right then to Bermuda. Avenue C hummed outside, it wasn't late, I wasn't hungry, I wasn't cold.

LIZARDS

IN THE MORNING I WENT UPTOWN INSTEAD OF DOWNTOWN PARTLY
because of habit and partly because of you. I sat on the steps of the
library for a while waiting for somebody to drop an ID card, the
way bums wait for swipes at the subway turnstiles, or Tom plucks
Met admission badges off the rotunda floor ("I don't owe them anything, I've given them my mother"). Nobody dropped one because
these are highly competent minor scholars carrying zippered wal-
lets in a variety of peach tones. They marched right into the library
as if going to the library were so easy. I went to your office.

You sat inside talking on the phone, and Barry and Carlo sat
outside in the hall. In a video game I would have had 2.5 seconds to
draw my ether pistol from the master belt I'd recently earned in the
Nether Woods and zap them for twenty points each, but I'd woken
up in real life at Mishti's, and carried only half a banana. I never
want more than half a banana, but I always want half a banana.
Bananas really back you up into a corner this way because all and
nothing are both unacceptable options. I saw the three yellow peel
parts flopping down over my jeans pocket and lifted the poor thing
to finish it. It was brown and mushy by now, and too much banana.
Barry and Carlo only noticed me by the sound the peel made hitting the bottom of the trash can between us.

"Nell, right?" Carlo asked. He could remember the name of his
girlfriend's professor's husband's visiting colleague, but not of her
best friend.

"Who are you?" I asked, showing him the masticated fruit in my mouth. Carlo neither answered nor laughed, confirming my total uselessness.

"Mr. Parada here is going to be helping out around the dean's office," Barry said. "Mendelson took an instant liking to him."

"Which shocked me, you know," Carlo looked less than shocked, "because I've heard Mendelson is a lizard."

It was five after nine in the morning and overnight new alliances had formed. I had only slept, Mishti had only sung, Barry had only burped I was sure since we'd met the afternoon before. Carlo had been in action.

"Well these guys never really want the administrative roles," Barry said. "It's an honor, and a bonus, so they take them for a term or two, but they need someone with a head like yours to execute."

Carlo dropped his shoulders and lengthened his neck, as if to emphasize that he had a head. I'd met guys like Carlo before, guys who had more means of executing their will than will, guys who lived therefore in a showroom of execution, their walls covered in thickly framed stock photography. I looked at Carlo and felt his brain operated inwardly—it wasn't love from others that fed him, it was a kind of problem solving that left him feeling clean and actual. Maybe he wouldn't suffocate Mishti after all. Maybe his distant father and fawning mother had left him suspicious and bored of love altogether. It was a shame he had such a great body. He might have been a circus star, had the determining forces of his childhood allowed for that as an outcome. He might have loved the way it felt to fall from a trapeze.

"*Nell*," you surprised all of us by being right there and speaking loudly, "for Christ's sake," you looked at your phone, "it's October third." I didn't know what to say, you were right. "Go home. Do you have a home?" You untied and retied the elastic at the bottom of your braid while I failed to answer this pretty difficult question. In mercy you kept going. "Finish your little reproductive interference piece by the fifteenth and we'll submit it to Oxford Systematic. You can do that in two weeks, you could do it in two days if you were functioning."

I wish so badly that I were functioning.

"Why would you want to interfere with reproduction?" Carlo asked.

I couldn't tell you that I would do it, because who knows if I'll really do it, and I didn't want to depress you with the likelihood that I wouldn't do it, and Barry was idly running his finger down a groove in your corduroys, and Carlo wasn't a trapeze artist, so I very strangely and slowly backed away.

"Nell?" you called. I could smell the banana peel in the trash. "The fifteenth?"

I just kept going, walking backwards like an idiot crab estranged from its own nature, and then down the stairs and then back to the library, where nobody had dropped anything of value.

SASSY BARK

THE NAME OF THIS BARK IS SASSY BARK. IT'S CATEGORIZED AS "AN ordeal." Joan! You are everywhere. You are the human of every plant. In West Africa all three kinds of *Erythrophleum*, the *suaveolens* and the *guineense* and the *chlorostachys*, produce the poisonous alkaloid erythrophleine, a toxic agent. In Liberia the relevant tradition is a trial by ordeal, in which a suspect drinks a whole lot of bark poison.

The person who is designated as guilty of the crime of witchcraft is arrested by the soldier king, and condemned to the ordeal of sassy-wood. The bark of the sassy-wood is powerfully narcotic, and a strong decoction of this the person condemned is forced to drink; and after he has drank it, he walks to and fro, exclaiming "Am I a witch," "am I a witch?" while one of his executioners walks behind him replying "You are a witch, you are a witch;" and this continues until he either throws off from his stomach the poison, when he is pronounced innocent, or it operates as a cathartic, when he is declared guilty, and compelled to take more of the decoction, and is subjected to other cruelties, which cause his speedy death.

James M. Connelly, "Report of the Kroo People," Appendix G, in Report of the Secretary of State, Communicating the Report of the Rev. R[alph] R[andolph] Gurley, Who Was Recently Sent Out by the Government to Obtain Information in Respect to Liberia, United States Senate, 31st Congress, 1st Session, Ex. Doc. No. 75, Washington, D.C., September 14, 1850, page 59

Now you just skipped over the citation but I wrote it out deliberately and I have to ask you to go back and look at it. I want you to understand that the reporter was Recently Sent Out by the Government to Obtain Information in Respect to Liberia. I want you to discover, the way I did, that R. R. stood for Ralph Randolph, and that Ralph couldn't hide that from posterity. We found out his secrets and put them in brackets. A civilized place to put them. Cane Sterling Professor Joan Kallas, Ecology Building Fourth Floor, [wedded a sleaze and can't find her way back to safety].

In terms of sassy's antidotes, I've found a classified ad for "various dry whole medicinal plants" in which an Italian retailer is looking for South American botanicals including maconha brava (*Zornia latifolia*) leaf. Maconha is the medicinal form of sassy. As far as I can tell, nobody has sold the Italian any maconha, but a Portuguese pharmaceutical company responded requesting information about the *Psychotria viridis* leaf the Italian is also hunting down. I would ideally like to crust the sassy bark in dried, crushed, and ground maconha powder, so the body receives both the benefit and the injury of the wood in one go.

This whole thing, if I could detoxify it by say 60 percent, would make a nice product. White chocolate peppermint bark for masochists. You'll tell me to finish a prototype by Christmas so we can sell it into the gift markets but all I want to do by Christmas is buy a lamp. And the more I stray from it, the more I want to go back to aconite. I think that's the entry point because it's straightforward and extensively tested and I can grow an herb box full of monkshood from seed starting next week. They'll bloom by summer. That's something I can do, something I even want to do.

For now I'm just down on my rugless floor admiring how totally democratic it was that the suspected witches were male, in nineteenth-century Africa. Those Liberian man-witches were not repressed. They pursued their craft, taking the word *witch* as their own, not even aspiring to *wizard*, even at the risk of suffering. It sucked if they got sassy-barked but the rest of the time they got to conjure whatever they wished. For a gender so boastful, very odd that Western men relinquish their claim to the practice of magic, very odd that they wouldn't yearn to be witches too.

Red Hook can turn into a carton of pastel cray-pas one hour before the sun goes down. The buildings are low enough, the water near enough, the sky wide and exposed, every kind of purple rises and stretches to pink. They come earlier and earlier, the purples, and with them a drop in temperature that makes night much more different from day than it used to be. I have to wear pants now. I'm surprised to find myself on the floor tonight, wearing pants. It does help to have the thin cushion of the cotton under me because the floor wood is so old and coated in grime. It's good here in my home tonight. I can make tortellini better because I have my colander. Until now I've been tilting the lid and tilting the pot and I always lose a couple and steam myself.

It's going to be okay, this solitude, this lovelessness, this school-lessness, this unstructure, this floating, this sinking. It's going to suit me. I'm going to mire in it until I'm cooked. Then, you know, I'll taste great. I just haven't cooked long enough, Joan. I just haven't been seasoned. Somewhere in my epicenter I am, I am, delicious. I'm going to lie alone on the floor here while the pinks stretch thin and darken (you asked if I had a home, you didn't ask if I had a bed, which would have been easier to answer, because I don't have a bed, who has a *bed* these days, you do) until one morning I wake up rested.

DRAGONS

TOM BUZZED MY INTERCOM WHILE I WAS STILL ON THE FLOOR ASLEEP in my pants. Mishti had given him my address, he said, and he wanted to see my "new situation." The comforting thing about this basically uncomfortable visit was that if I had answered the door naked, it would have felt the same. The almost of it, which is the most irresistible part of anything, leads to a simple body yes or no and when it came to me and Tom the *almost* always asked itself and the *no* always reverberated. *No!* we silently shouted at each other, each time our genitals came near. Once that's been answered, nothing is tantalizing. I noticed that the left side of my chin was crusted in dried drool as I unchained the door and that was fine too.

"Welcome."

"Well Nell, look here, you've landed."

"Have I?"

"I'd say."

Sometimes we spoke in British accents to mock his forbears.

"You've even got a bathroom sink."

I joined him in my minuscule bathroom, peered around his arm into the mirror, and removed the drool from my chin. It felt good to stand with him in such a small room, it felt like being held.

"I've got a sink in the kitchen too," I said, "and a refrigerator."

"You don't say."

"No dish soap yet."

"Don't get greedy."

"No bath towels."

"No bed?"

"No bed."

Tom smiled and said, "Who has a *bed* these days?" and I could hear my own voice in his voice. We'd been very good friends. We'd shared a little lingo. The fact of there being no bed now was an additional comfort to us, as it removed even that opportunity for awkwardness. He walked around my castor bean pot to the windows.

"At least the view."

"At most, really."

"It took me a very long time to get here."

"About as far as Litchfield."

"Veronica sends condolences," Tom joined his palms, "on our love."

"My best to her."

It was okay that Tom had come, but I didn't know why he'd bothered. I lived, as he'd said, an hour and a half south of the Upper East Side in a neighborhood that didn't have a single Pick-A-Bagel. He looked restless and weird and must have wanted something from someone.

"Have you ever met Joan's mother?" Tom asked.

"There it is," I said.

"What?"

"Nothing. No, I haven't, she passed away, but I've met her father."

"Where?" He seemed to want to ask, *How? Why? When? Me too?*

"You know they run a diner—"

"I didn't know. I don't know why you would think that I would know."

"That Viand on 82nd, it's near you. Her father is still behind the cake counter. Kostas, short for Konstantinos, which was incidentally the name of Joan's dead cat. Her dad is original 1970s New York Greek diner stock. He's got to be almost eighty."

"Your command of Kallas trivia frightens me."

"It's funny because she's the opposite of a ten-page spiral-bound menu. She is exactly not a cheesecake."

"But is she a spinach pie?"

It was over now, he'd asked and I'd bragged and I considered the interaction complete. I wondered how best to dismiss him. It seemed cruel because he'd transferred from the 4 to the 6 to the F. You would have known how to dismiss him immediately.

Tom said, "Can I ask you something?"

Maybe it was just that I knew he would open the can up right then.

"Must you?"

"I must. What is the Joan thing with you?"

"Do you want to rephrase that?"

"What is your thing with Joan? I wanted to ask while we were together but in that context it seemed . . . aggressive. Now I'm just curious. I'm allowed."

A warm blank weather took up the space in my head and I felt ferociously calm.

I thought about clouds and said, "I don't know, I like to know her, I like to please her, I would report the weather to Joan if I could."

"You could."

"Well, I would."

Tom shifted his weight around a little and played with his own thumb.

"I wanted to say there's something Greek about it," he said, "but I didn't know that she's literally Greek. But yeah, it feels . . . almost religious."

I thought about this and said, "Yes, I'm devoted."

"Religious but not romantic?"

"I want to serve her," I said. "Is that romantic?"

"It can be?"

"Yeah I guess it could. It's just not the focus. Romance. It's never been my focus."

Tom made a face that said, *It's always been my focus.*

And then I think we both agreed to stop. Tom studies dragons, I study the venom compounds inside a dragon's tooth, and that's the whole divide. Our overlap is that you are the dragon.

As he walked down my stairs Tom said, "Maybe she wants it."

"What?"

"Romantic devotion."

I couldn't think of anything to say and he left the building, as if to mount his horse. It was a mild, clear morning. I got a chill all through my arm hair and registered that my way of life would soon be substantially threatened.

COOKIES

"A IS FOR ACONITE," YOU SAID IN COOKIE MONSTER'S VOICE, A gross misuse of a voice I usually love.

"Bite me."

"Cool it."

"Dig a trench."

"Enough."

"Fuck you."

"That was too easy, Nell."

"Fine. Forget it."

"Good."

"How's Barry."

"I don't know."

"Joan always knows."

"Knows what?"

"Love. Men."

"Never."

"Oh."

"Please."

"Question or command?"

"Really neither."

"So, please what?"

"Take a hike."

"Upstate?"

"Vermont. Wherever."

"Xanadu?"

"Your pick."

"Zesty," I concluded, as if jumping into a swimming pool wearing your best fur. You smiled your rare smile because we were jerks who'd gone all the way. Tom will never satisfy you! I left rejoicing. Tom stops at T. I didn't even blow any dust out of your name. I went straight home victorious to submit nothing to Oxford Systematic Biology.

CONQUEROR

AFTER YOU GOT OVER MY MISSING THAT DEADLINE, YOU GAVE ME A packet of High John the Conqueror roots. Mishti and I planted them on Halloween. She brought a couple herbal remedy books down to Red Hook, some her mother's, some her own. I had a few as well. It's hard not to think in terms of remedies when you spend time planting things, because it's so absolutely supernatural that anything grows.

In addition to the Conqueror, I had dandelion, clover, and some masterwort. Masterwort flowers look like the fireworks the child princess of Sweden would set off on her fifth birthday. A burst of tiny pink dots surrounded by a lion's head of long white tear-shaped petals. They are in the same family as carrots. Mishti brought me two presents she'd ordered from MountainRoseHerbs.com: dragon's blood resin and myrrh gum resin, because she was in the resin department and myrrh with cinnamon is supposed to be strengthening. She'd decided to spend some of her bloated P&G internship wages at Union Market on cinnamon sticks, bay leaves, dried red mulberries, lemon mint, plantains, a peach, and two heads of ginger. She came in praising the very good flower man on Degraw Street who'd sold her such irises and sunflowers.

I'd purchased a couple red plastic planters from the Ace Hardware and a whole bunch of dirt. We spread garbage bags out over the floor and sat on them. The dirt sacks kept falling over. Mishti opened *Cunningham's Encyclopedia of Magical Herbs* and *New-*

comb's Wildflower Guide between our legs. It was Halloween night, we were living in a semi-enlightened society, nobody would sassy-bark us, there was no reason not to get witchy.

I had spent the month very slowly but somewhat comprehensively reviewing basic herbal properties. Mishti's understanding of organic chemistry is so profound I didn't want to embarrass myself by volunteering my mushy little speculations, my far-fetched goals, but I knew she could guide us if we started violating any natural orders.

We lit a couple of those Magic Hour candles that even the most secular shops are selling now, though Mishti said they included all the wrong essences. ("Like, why even bother with Angelica blossom.") We had the purple Spirit one, the yellow Home one, and the orange Vitality. We also had four huge, blank, and vaguely phallic votives I'd purchased for 79 cents each at IKEA, the day I bought my lamp. We had a king-size bag of Cheetos to make our fingers orange (extra vitality) and a jar of raw honey to spread over our cheeks. I definitely don't know what we were doing but even you would have admitted we were *doing* something. Also you would love my lamp. It's ugly, tall, stoic, and super bright.

The castors I'd planted a month earlier were still deeply invisible but I wanted to believe I could smell them beginning to exist. We worked with a wormwood cutting I was trying to re-pot and nestled it between the dandelion and pipsissewa in one long planter. Pipsissewa usually fails to germinate from seed, but we tried anyway because that wormwood-dandelion-pip trio is recommended for calling spirits. I agree this was reckless of us, because we didn't even know which spirits we wanted to call. I thought we would choose retroactively. Cunningham's suggestion for attaining "success" is lemon balm, clover, ginger, High John the Conqueror, rowan, wahoo, and Winter's bark. We had everything except the last three, which promised us 57 percent success, which is the most any responsible person could expect.

Cucumber hinders lust. Its peel bound onto the forehead relieves headache pain (Mishti usually has one) and the seeds promote fertility. This lustless, painless, fertile condition seemed attractive to us so we fashioned cucumber-peel headbands and collected a few seeds in a tumbler. Aspen, caraway, cumin, juniper, garlic, and vetiver work together to prevent theft, so we threw a clove and some ripped-up rye bread and the ground spice into the glass of cucumber seeds and drenched it all with gin and took turns drinking from it while rubbing each other's bellies, even though there is exactly nothing to steal here. I would mourn if this notebook were stolen. I expect it will be. The city is full of Marion Hawthornes to my Harriet, though if Marion read this particular notebook aloud she'd find it understimulating, seeing as she isn't you.

We cut Mishti's peach into wedges and filled the bottom of a vase with them. We stuck the sunflower and iris stalks one by one into the fleshes of the peach. These three together promote wisdom. We had no bladder wrack to raise the wind. The dragon's blood resin is supposed to be used by "women seated near an open window, looking outside, at night." We did that. This resin is high in taspine, an alkaloid for tissue and skin regeneration, quick to seal wounds and stop bleeding, and it may be something I can use as an anti-toxin. Mishti doesn't know what good taste she has in bad gifts and I didn't tell her. She said one ounce had cost her ten dollars. I realized I'd never afford as much as I'd need. We took off our cucumber headbands and ate them.

Three of our candles blew out at the same time and we took that as a sign to go to Sunny's. It's just one block over and coincidentally the best bar in Brooklyn. You will never see it, the way I will never see the inside of Jean-Georges. I think you are missing more but I am eating less. It's mostly that I wish you could know what dodgy industrial Brooklyn feels like on a muggy night full of nothing but paint and seawater, just as you wish you could show me Barry's family's summer home in Palm Beach, the light falling on Riverside Drive, the best of things. Just as I wish you wished. In any case Sunny's has a painting of a palm tree hanging over the gin shelves, so there's some continuity.

Mishti entered the bar with her head thrown so far back, and her shoulders so proud and wide, she looked like a high school football player in his graduation photo. I looked like her water boy. Sunny himself passed away about a year ago and they've been rotating new bartenders—I don't know any of their names. They don't know mine. Everybody knows Mishti's. She's been there once.

"Tequila, Mishti?" someone said. She confirmed and he poured it for her free of charge. I asked for a whiskey soda and he charged me $7.50. Mishti sat on a high stool laughing at me, her shawl pouring from her shoulders to the floor like whitewater. I was wearing a hat inside and I couldn't say why.

Mishti took her shot, wiped her mouth, and said, "Barry's the devil." We hadn't been talking about Barry, I hadn't put her up to it, she was simply and unilaterally offering me this kindness.

"Please sir may I have some more!"

"He just waits around outside after class and jumps on whoever comes out first. And I always come out first because Joan's laser-gunning me with her fucking eyebrows by the end of class and I have to basically seek shelter. And then Barry goes, *Something something nucleus!* and I have to laugh and then he's *so happy* I'm laughing."

"You don't have to laugh."

"But he's like . . . really *pleasant*. He just wiggles, pleasantly, at me. It's hard to meet that with unpleasantness because he's having such a nice time."

She stared into her empty shot glass and remembered about the devil.

"It's gross," she said, "because then he does it all over again to anyone else."

"You want his wiggles for your own."

She did and she was embarrassed so she said, "No, I want him to stop wiggling."

"Amen."

"And he does it with this look in his eyes like he's just waiting for one crumb, waiting for me to drop one crumb so he can just eat it, really eat it up, like a maniac."

"And you've never dropped one?"

"I have total control," Mishti said, "and he will never touch me." She looked into the dead center of my eyeballs and said, "He's disgusting."

She wanted to leave it there so we did. The bartender refilled her shot. I didn't order another drink because I didn't need one and I couldn't pay for it.

"When does the school end your stipend," I asked, "never?"

"I don't know, I just try to stay enrolled."

"I need a stipend."

"Bartend."

The palm tree lit up above my head.

"Tony," I said. Nobody answered. "Pete." "Asher." "Nathaniel."

If you can believe it, the bartender's name was Nathaniel.

"Yeah?" he looked at me. In his glance I understood that he wanted me to stop talking and his name was probably George.

I moved my head so it was closer to his head, punched both my elbows down onto the bar hitting both funny bones, and with little shocked tears in my eyes asked, "Hire me?" Most of my body was over the bar now, I was lying on it, on my stomach. "I've just spent my last fifteen dollars on seven candles and a whiskey and I'd like to restock my stocks. I live around the corner. I can work weird hours."

"Ask Johansen," he said, unblinking.

I pictured becoming the newest anonymous employee, I would no longer need to know my own name, I would even be willing to give Mishti her drinks for free, as she'd come to expect, and to charge myself.

George shouted, "Hey Johansen." A blond woman stood. I peeled my torso off the bar and hurried to pick the peanut shells out of my sweater. Mishti took her second shot and slammed the glass down, taking credit.

FEVERFEW

I DON'T KNOW WHAT HAPPENED AFTER THAT NIGHT, THERE WAS
something I'd liked the taste of, I failed three martini tests but I
passed the fourth and started working, I used my tip money on
seed packets. I went a little nuts. I bought enough planters to fill my
empty apartment. I bought enough dirt to bury myself. I've been so
focused on poisonous plants, it proved extremely therapeutic to
plant safe, moral flowers. I planted cowslip and bupleurum and
mizuna and yellow rattle. Everlasting sweet pea and Harlequin
sweet pea. Stereo broad beans and sweet cicely. Mishti came over
to study for your midterm while I planted garlic and set it out beside the nightshade on the fire escape. I bought single-tier LED
grow lights that aren't lab grade but make do. I know most of the
flowers will fail. Some of them will love blooming. I put larkspur
between the Johnny-jump-ups and the feverfew. Sometimes I'd
light a votive next to only one planter to make it feel some particular encouragement and care. I had a sense that it would soon be
very cold, colder than I or anything could tolerate. When I went to
pee at night I kicked fourteen planters. I never turned on the lights
and I eventually understood where to walk to avoid them. My toes
are still busted up. My apartment looks like a corn maze for chin-
chillas. The first shoots are going to bloom in March in April in
May. They're going to be twenty colors. Tom and Mishti took your
midterm. The sweet pea is good for strength and the dandelion is
good for wish manifestation. Johansen has me working the mid-

night to five a.m. shift because I'm being put in my place. I feel jet-lagged from noon to midnight but I've been jet-lagged since I got expelled. The money is bad but absolutely adequate. Mishti doesn't come to see me at the bar because she's a highly competent minor scholar who needs her sleep. I would have given her the bar for free. I walk to and from work with a Bic lighter in my pocket so that if somebody starts mugging me I can at least light it up and see my mugger's face. Muggers have cool faces. I can't wait for the cowslip to bloom. Cowslip on your stoop will discourage visitors. Also known as password, peggle, plumrocks. Source of healing, source of appetite, source of treasure-finding.

CHEESE

THE WEEK BEFORE ACTUAL THANKSGIVING, THE ECOLOGY EVOLUTION & Environmental Biology Department celebrated Thanksgiving in the faculty lounge. I hadn't yet been removed from their email list and that made me feel less excommunicated. The department wanted to make it clear that this gathering was a favor and an inconvenience, and asked us not to bring any partners. The goal of the party was that it should seem, pretty much immediately afterward, that there never had been any party.

New York has put up with an ultra-cold November and we arrived in our winter clothes, bulk the faculty lounge wasn't built to accommodate. There weren't any coat hooks but we also weren't supposed to put our coats on the chairs. They asked that we remove our shoes. We made a coat pile on the floor, to the left of the shoe pile. We'd known about no partners, but none of us had anticipated the shoe rule, a rule that left everyone shorter and stumpy-looking. Mishti wore extra-long, extra-wide woolen sailor pants that relied entirely on her platform boots. She now looked like a broom. Tom's socks were one orange one purple. I was miserably and idiotically not wearing socks. I walked around even more hesitantly than usual, afraid that I was infecting the carpet with my toenail fungus.

You were perfect in black tights, black tunic, gray braid. You looked at my toenails with a face that said, *You're a donkey*. It seemed like a very dirty trick to return midterms the day of the Thanksgiving party, not giving anyone anywhere to hide or recover, but you hate hiding and recovery. Tom had come for the mulled wine, with the ease of a pass/fail student who'd just passed. The B- you gave Mishti has changed her life. I've never seen her cry in public, because she doesn't like the chemicals that make water-proof mascara waterproof and isn't interested in making a mess, but she was inconsolable. She'd worn her platforms as armor and even they had been taken away from her.

I wished that she'd been able to bring Carlo, his height would have been a kind of shield and given her a wall to lean against, but no partners meant no Carlo and no Barry, and no Barry made the party worthwhile. Without Barry you are comically incapacitated at social functions. He is your mouth, your hand, your laughter. You stood by the mulled wine crockpot apparently focused on smelling it. I came over to get some.

You didn't greet me in any way so I poured first and then said, "Professor Kallas."

"Bartender," you said.

I was about to launch into a heavy-handed diatribe about peo-ple who need to earn a living and people who get by being wealth-adjacent, but Tom came and spared me the humiliation.

"Professor Kallas," he also said.

To this you responded with great warmth. "Tell Francesca we're stealing you," you said. I hated Francesca and didn't know who she was.

Tom was so flattered he nearly fainted, and then I saw him col-lect and steel himself. His natural state is mid-faint, and it takes a lot of effort on his part to concentrate, but when he does, his focus is arresting. It's the cloud eyes. He's got such inviting, colorless cloud eyes.

It was only when you added, "*I mean it*," a flirty redundancy you never stoop to, that I realized you'd been there setting up for two hours and were deeply and seriously drunk. The little decline of your chin you'd performed to give the phrase extra verve made you lose your balance and you wobbled to straighten yourself. You weren't looking at me, you weren't aware of me, you weren't even trying to insult me, you were simply attracted to Tom. All at once I was sad, as if I'd walked up to some roadkill.

Tom strapped on his helmet and ran right onto the playing field. "I'll tell Francesca I'm already gone," he said. "I'm sure she knows, anyway."

This wasn't zingy enough for you, it took him too long to get the words out, and by "anyway" you'd become distracted by the increasingly Pisa-like coat pile. I stepped up to take my turn.

"Your name means a muddy place," I said.

"That's the Polish spelling."

"If you two got married," Tom said, looking at us, "your combined name would be Jello. That could be your wedding hashtag, #jelloshots."

I started to think we were all drunker than we understood.

Tom stood there chuckling at himself, and even though you find the word *hashtag* unlawful, you looked entertained by his chuckling. He asked if you'd tried any of the cheeses and you said you hadn't. Of course you hadn't. I thought of the pepper-jack cubes stacked high at Rachel's funeral reception. Then, wordlessly, the two of you walked to the cheese table.

I—

If there's a pillar in your life, it's worth removing it. Break down your life and see what broke. If you were to imagine the three most essential elements of your days and then imagine your days without them, what comes rushing to take their place? It's so quiet when you bust down your acoustic paneling. Sometimes the body wants to be burned and sometimes it doesn't; self-neglect isn't infinite it's cyclical, as self-care is. Every time you get to a binary choice there's a third. Have you ever walked out with nothing to give but your innermost energy? Have you ever been nothing other than a crayon? We don't love most of the people we love. You're not who you thought I was.

What is it that I want from you? Do I want to press the corner of your mouth into your mouth? Do I want to hold the back of your neck as if you'd been injured? Do I want to steam up your eyeballs with my breath? How long until I am the recipient of my own discoveries and not their messenger? I deliver everything I am to you. I stood there by the crockpot and let a wall of air push through the room of myself. I have never exhibited sexuality only competence. I will make myself eggs for dinner. You will love my French toast. I will never invite you over for it. You will come for comfort, for company. I never need company. I have as much as I need.

There was one final patch of late-falling red leaves on the maple across the street, the light was now too dim to see, and I could feel it pulsing there, wanting to be lit up again, like anyone. I had followed you to the cheese table during my spin-out. You were in the middle of saying to Tom, "She missed the Oxford. It was publishable."

I said, "The publishing thing is your tenure problem, you know, not mine."

"It will be yours if you're lucky."

"It makes me want to scratch my skin off when you suggest something boring to me."

"Pass/fail students shouldn't come to the party," Mishti said, bringing us to a boil. I hadn't seen her walking toward us. She looked unwell.

You said, "Maybe admission should be an A."

I knew then that you were legitimately interested in Tom, that it was happening. Only real tenderness inspires your most random and needless cruelty.

Mishti officially snapped and said, "Maybe I should accept your husband's dinner invitation."

You said, "I'd like him out of the house Thursday night."

Tom said, "He invited you to dinner?"

Mishti said, "Why do the jerk-offs get to join your club, it's like you have to be lazy, or gross, or expelled. Like why does Nell still get to be your sidekick? She fucked it up."

"Nell's very good," you said, so blankly and harshly I thought I'd misheard you. "Nell completed enough work after three years to qualify for her doctorate right then, which makes the situation all the more laughable. She's been at PhD level for years but now she'll never be one." You actually went so far as to point your finger at Mishti's face. "You're more able but she works harder."

I ate a cheese. I ate two more cheeses. I couldn't speak or join you in the wild gift you were giving, because when you walked away with Tom I'd dug myself into a grave of self-reliance, and I hadn't brought a ladder, and I stood stuck down there, confused.

The truth is that I worked kind of pathologically hard when I started this program and nobody has ever known that—not my parents in the Midwest, not my very few friends—I didn't even realize you'd known it. I didn't need a pat on the head and didn't get one, but the work did make me elementally tired later in a way nobody could justify and therefore came across as crabbiness. Your patience with me these past two years now felt radically informed, just, and loving.

Mishti retreated to the mulled wine. What I found most surprising about this altogether surprising exchange was the insinuation that she didn't work hard enough. I'd known Mishti to be a marching band, exact and coordinated and unstoppable. You were separating competence from some looser sort of vision. It was a shame that vision, when it occurred, was inevitably so loose, so often useless, so much less visible than something complete and unoriginal. I think you were wrong about both of us: Mishti can be wildly inventive even within the rigidities of her excellence and I am finger-painting. But this was a kindness you paid me, the first and I expect the last, and I'll never give it away, or back to you.

The night soon ended. We found our coats in the pile. Nobody could bear to be in the same room anymore. We'd eaten too much cheese and needed to use our own bathrooms. It was only seven o'clock. Beautiful heavy snow had begun to fall and we wished it hadn't. We put on our boots, all our respective boots, and went out into it.

DECEMBER

"We lived long together
   a life filled,
         if you will,
with flowers. So that
   I was cheered
         when I came first to know
that there were flowers also
         in hell."

WILLIAM CARLOS WILLIAMS

SWEET POTATOES

I FIRST TURNED TO BOTANY LIKE ANYBODY DOES BECAUSE I FOUND flowers terrifyingly attractive and had been raised by reasonable people who didn't put beauty at the center of their lives. I thought I could put it there.

Now the study of beauty and how it grows has become my work, and I think that's the best way of keeping it. But it also leaves the door open for something else to fill in the beauty-as-beauty center. The useless beauty. The not work. And I think what is really useless is the way I love you. I want to put that in the center.

One example of non-uselessness is how I filled up that first notebook. I didn't expect to get to the end of it, maybe because I believed you when you said I'd never do anything ever again. But today I had to put on public-facing butt-hushing outdoor pants and go out and buy a second book from the bodega man, you'll see I've even maxed out the margins of the first one. I've always admired my particular bodega man for carrying black-and-white Compositions behind the register, and one box of blue ballpoint pens, as if they were treats people might like to buy on a Thursday with loose cash. I also bought a strawberry Yoo-hoo. Having drunk the sixteen fluid ounces of milk beverage in one gulp I commence now a new notebook, a night season. I'll call this notebook December. We haven't had a storm since Thanksgiving, but between storms the darkness lies like a little snow over the streets.

Day and night the city's electronic flakes never fall. These four-foot glow-in-the-dark geometries dangle overhead, threatening to impale the holiday. There are so many attractive, ambitious, well-dressed people in this city with well-shaped arms and goals and for the next four months they'll be invisible under their parkas. We'll all be walking eyes, impossibly equal to each other, and then my castor plant will bloom.

I'm writing this behind the bar. I ended the last notebook with Cheese and that's where you praised me so I'm sticking to only edible titles in this book. I don't know what to call this one, so far we've only got Yoo-hoo. A woman's sitting at the bar with good posture. She keeps looking to see if I have become the person she's hoping will arrive. I'm still anonymous. Sometimes I make a little noise with my shaker to remind her that she nevertheless isn't entirely alone. She ordered one chardonnay half an hour ago and hasn't drunk any of it. I'd like to refill it for her but she'll have to make a little progress first. Mishti isn't here to keep the pours flowing, she's out on a date with your husband. She looks really, really great. She's wearing the top of a purple sari and pink jeans and some extraordinarily fancy earrings that hang down to her beefy shoulders.

What you underestimated about Mishti is her thoroughness: when you said *Thursday night* she went exponential to *every Thursday night*. What have you been doing on your Thursday nights, Professor Kallas? I haven't come near you since you praised me because I want to ride it a little longer. The next thing you say to me will be so rude, wisely, in the name of balance, that I won't be able to trust or enjoy the memory of your praise anymore. Right now I can be Jasmine (talk about pants) on this soft carpet you wove me and fly above the city alone because I am *also* Aladdin, the thief. I get both seats on your carpet.

Chardonnay just looked up from her totally full glass and told me I ought to be a psychologist. I asked her why. She said because I'm willing to wait. Everybody's always rushing her, she said, I don't make her feel rushed. She said I have a patient face.

I told her that I've never expected very much to happen. Easy to wait when there's nothing to wait for. She said, Oh, you'd be shocked by the things that happen. To ordinary people. They'll tell you stories to melt your head. I said, *Melt your head?* When you're their shrink, she said.

Chardonnay then abruptly settled her tab and left, so I'm drinking her glass, Merry Christmas. Joan the Christmas rose has another name, it's hellebore. Nobody has ever been stupid enough to say "hella" in your presence not even in 2001 and I don't think roses are boring so we can call it Christmas rose to be festive. It's blooming now. I bloomed one on my kitchen windowsill. What a menace! The sap is a skin irritant and one medicinal dose of it killed Alexander the Great. The leaves, though, are deep and lustrous and the blossoms are unfathomably maroon. I've grown it for your office so that you have a little seasonal weapon on hand next time Barry and Carlo come to play. Barry is a balding Alexander and Carlo's skin has never, not once, been irritated. You being you, what you'll love most is the foliage green so dark it approaches black.

There was a Wednesday five years ago when I'd nowhere to go for Christmas, the Wednesday was Christmas Eve. It was my first year in the graduate program. I went to the student center to collect my mail but I hadn't gotten any mail, so I was just standing in the student center. You rushed in to leave a couple graded papers in mailboxes. You saw me standing there, *Mabberley's Plant-Book* about to fall from my elbow. What I remember best—I don't even remember what we ate for dinner that night, aside from the sweet potatoes—is how long it took you to speak, and how oddly and patiently you waited for yourself to decide what to do about me. We are neither of us inherently *social*. We stood parallel to each other, both facing the mailboxes, but I could feel you reading me in your periphery, and I stood very still because I wanted to be read. Then you said, "Where are you from?"

I knew who you were, I'd applied to Columbia to study with you. Like a brat I said, "Kansas, Professor Kallas."

You said, "Assistant Professor."

I said your breakdown of leaf trait evolution was the single most inspired and inspiring work of contemporary botany I'd ever read. You explained that your boyfriend's cousins were coming over for dinner and that you wished painful deaths upon them. Your boyfriend's name was Barry. I'd probably met him as a counselor at freshman orientation. I said I had. You said he always encouraged *student interaction* and that you'd openly avoided it but that this time he'd approve. I think you actually called me a *charitable case*. I promised to sit between you and cousin four. You took me, quietly, efficiently, home.

That was your old apartment in Astoria. You were thirty-five and I was twenty-five and I was so impressed by your fortitude, your magnitude, by the apartment you rented alone as if living alone in New York were possible. By the authority of your blank walls and the unheard-of oranges striping the thin, not warm, and very sophisticated quilt on your bed. By the ceiling-high walnut shelf of multicolored encyclopedias, itself a jumbo encyclopedia of encyclopedias, that sternly faced your bed and must have been the first and last thing you saw each day. By the one little St. Bernard's lily growing on your windowsill and the cat who nibbled at it. I wanted immediately, with my whole self, to be your cat.

You took me, in your equalizing uninflected way, entirely seriously. You let me peel the sweet potatoes. You introduced me to Barry as "a botanist." I'd only told you as the N train crossed the Queensboro Bridge that I wanted to study the harshest grossest facts about the world's prettiest organisms. You'd nodded at that as if I'd said I needed to use the bathroom, something basic and inevitable about my body. I think the bottom line is that we're very similar.

Barry (very different) proposed with a princess-cut gray diamond that New Year's Eve and by the following Christmas you'd moved into Riverside Drive. I declined your repeat invitation, which I still believe was a relief to you. It's cute to have a student in the mix in Astoria. It's weird to dilute Riverside Drive with me.

I'd spent the year reading everything I thought you'd ever read, so that I could speak to you. I didn't want to sit across from you at a dinner table, I wanted us to coauthor a grafting treatise. You were always working on a paper of your own because the department had laid its tenure hoops out before you and asked you to start jumping. Still you read my abstracts and poked the right holes in them. Sometimes you'd ask my opinion of something we'd both read. I learned my own opinions by giving them to you. I did my own work and you did yours and in that way you and I grew older for a good couple of years.

The person who believes in you is the most dangerous person

you know. The person who believes in you can unbuild you in an instant. We haven't learned how to curb that danger. We don't know what to do with the person who names our life. The one who says *Do this, right now, not that* and the *this* that person casually suggests becomes your entire livelihood. The one who lends you a hat that allows you to enter a room. A coat to survive your own winter. We don't know how to thank, because gratitude is traded in sexual currency. If you don't marry the person you're most grateful to, if you don't fuck them or pretend you want to, the part of you that person created shrivels a little. The part of me you created has overtaken the rest of me, as a weed, because all I do is thank you, is thank you, is thank you.

It isn't as if you aren't beautiful, you are beautiful. It isn't as if you don't find me, in whatever way you find me, beautiful. It's that our interest in each other is a cold lake and neither of us wants to jump in. We want to stand together, at the edge of the cold lake.

Maybe I ought to become a psychologist. Maybe I ought to melt my own head.

The splendid thing is that right now, as I write, all the heat in the world has collected in the bread basket that sits between my best friend and your husband. Between Mishti's vigor, and Barry's lust, their combined temperatures could maybe warm us, maybe even at this distance.

TACOS

"NO, CARLO DOESN'T *KNOW* ABOUT IT."

"Keeping secrets is basically apologizing. You hate apologizing."

"There's no *it* for him to know about. A taco dinner is not a secret."

"How about three taco dinners?"

Mishti had reversed herself so completely it was almost as if nothing had changed. Perhaps dating her nemesis made the most perfect sense. Perhaps anything made more sense than dating Carlo. I'm leaving the fate of your marriage aside.

"I'm not *dating Barry*," she said, as if in response to the things I hadn't said aloud. She knew how it looked. "I'm just figuring him out. If I can figure out what Joan sees in Barry, maybe I'll finally understand how she thinks. I'll ace her final," Mishti said. "At the very least I'll have taken something from her."

Mishti, who I think of as authentically powerful, now needed to wield that power over *you*, needed *you* to recognize it, needed her enemy's surrender, to prove her knack for victory. It's the same thing I went through, but more glamorous—her story confident, mine meek. Anyway, all roads lead to whatever: she'll soon need your nearness to confirm her basic existence, like I do, like Tom is realizing he will.

"You won't figure anything out," I told her. "And you're not taking anything, Barry's giving it away. Besides, Joan doesn't see anything in Barry, there's something else going on."

"What else can go on in a marriage?"

"I don't know but it isn't vision."

"You can't think it's only the money. Very unlike you."

"It's not the money but it's something about the way the money made her feel once when she was younger."

Mishti didn't respond, we were curled up under the library's grand staircase, deep in a hollow triangle that formed underneath the first flight. It was so dark I couldn't see Mishti at all but I could feel her clothing on my arm and it was soft in an otherworldly way. She was trying to think about how money made her feel, being young.

While she thought about it I closed my eyes and drew a little evolutionary food chain parade across my eyelids: Mishti, wunderkind, 26; Nell, *Homo sapiens*, 31; Carlo, half-machine, 35; Joan, sorceress, 41; Barry, troll, 45. Tom wasn't in the food chain because centaurs don't eat or get eaten.

Then Mishti said, "He likes the way I look at him."

"Barry?"

"Which is, you know, to be avoided, because if he likes being looked at he's either narcissistic or neglected and the former lasts forever and the latter eventually heals and turns into cruelty as a kind of historical payback."

"Do you like the fact that he thinks about you? Does that make you think about you?"

"At least he thinks about me, at least he isn't one of the dreamies—"

"Dreamies?"

"Who use eccentricity and neediness as a mask for extreme solipsism and hopes for social ascension—"

"We're back to Tom now?"

"Or dudes who love their brother. That's the worst. The brother-best-friend club. Totally toxic."

I realized that Mishti had been dating since she was thirteen years old and had been born symmetrical and had understood more about her own body and sexuality at age seven than I did today. She could, at a glance, provide a man's kingdom, phylum, class, order, family, genus, and species. I pictured her standing beside Linnaeus, both of them wearing white curly eighteenth-century wigs. Mishti would say to him, "Hey Carl," and he'd coo, "*Ja* Mishti," and show her his Swedish flowers. Incidentally can you imagine being sent on a journey through Sweden in 1740 to classify the planet's plants and animals? Can you imagine his boots?

I wanted to end this tolerating and aggrandizing of Barry's libido. "He sees you as an augmentation of his reality. His reality," I repeated because Mishti was almost certainly doing something to her own fingernails and not listening in any way. "The focus is his reality and what you do to it. Not love."

Tom's face came back to me, the face he'd made when I said romance wasn't my focus. I'd given him permission, right then, to ruin my life. I can't believe he commenced his great romance at the cheese table.

"I'd like it," I said to Mishti, venting some misplaced retroactive anger at Tom, "if you could find a way to measure your own self-worth without praise from other people. Forget Joan, forget Barry, forget me, just go home to yourself."

"*Forget Joan*, she says. What a load of hypocrite shit."

Mishti won every argument in this way. She had for the past five years. Her vanity was untouchable because of my obsession.

She knew I loved you, she knew I loved you too much, she knew I didn't know why or how or what to do about it, she knew it was an exhaust pipe for every private tension I carried, she knew you didn't love me, and she loved me, and knew me well, and wanted to protect me from the disappointment of something I didn't understand.

I felt her fabric pull away from me and the minute thuds of her knees crawling forward. Then she was out of our hole and I could see her calves and ankles in silhouette. I gave her a minute to make her exit and then crawled out myself—sometimes sitting under the staircase alone is a good idea but it usually isn't. Someone had opened one of the library's grand windows and its long curtain billowed out into the room. It was so smooth and pregnant I wanted to take a picture of it, but should anyone be allowed to take a picture of a window curtain full of wind, stealing and stabilizing its motion? Why celebrate it by robbing it of the very thing you're celebrating? And what is a photograph of love, is it marriage?

My phone was dead anyway so I stood and celebrated the curtain in my mind. I don't even know if you know about Mishti and Barry. I don't even know what I know about you and Tom. I'm going to go home to myself now. I'm going to take my own medicine and go home.

CREAM

YOU OPENED YOUR OFFICE DOOR AND SAID, "CLOSED."

"What was all of that about my being 'very good'?"

You let me in. I only then realized I'd gone home to your office.

"Well I've done the math and calculated that you stopped being very good right when you started dating Tom."

"So?"

"So I want to see what it feels like," you said with a sardonic twist to your mouth I'd never seen before, "I want to fuck off and see how it feels. It's not something I've ever done before." The idea of you *fucking off* made me imagine first the sun finally exploding, second malnutrition, and third some kind of miniature vibrator that made me sadly horny.

"So what have you been doing?" I asked, hoping very much you wouldn't tell me. Please don't tell me what you and Tom are doing. "Ice skating?"

"Yes. Every Thursday night we go ice skating."

"And what's with the Thursdays did you and Barry write a Thursday clause into your marriage—"

"You were right about Mishti, give her a command and she executes."

"She executes your marriage."

"With a hot pink guillotine."

"Tom isn't the right dude to end a marriage for, even yours," I was stooping so low now my tongue touched the floor, "he's not really interested in taking care of anybody."

"I'm not ending anything Nell you alarmist librarian. I'm beginning the part of my life in which I like living."

Because I am interested in taking care of you, or at least, because I care about you, aggressively, I want you to like living. I know you have low self-esteem but I think you have perfect self-knowledge. You have the grown woman's gift of preferences—you want Weil over De Beauvoir; your skin wants acid, not serum; you wake up with a single cumulus cloud of inertia filling your entire head and you want fatty cream in your coffee; you want a lot of salt; your shape is this shape and calls for that pant leg; you have chosen your field of work and every day you choose it; your oil is this oil, your fruit this fruit, you tolerate lactose and grain—these aren't questions anymore, only a laborious set of rules you follow to satisfy your own demands. I guess I've assumed that kind of internal fluency would make days easier.

"I never thought of you as unhappy," I said, as if you'd insulted me.

"Do you think of yourself as unhappy?"

"No." But I have no demands and I don't know myself very well.

"Well, we're the same," you said, in a warm almost whisper, and with that tranquilizer in my system I climbed back on your flying carpet and hovered out of your office, down the stairs, into some afternoon rain.

Barry rushed up to catch the door from me, shaking out his umbrella. He looked terrified and wet, as if he hadn't been holding his umbrella over his head but somewhere else.

"Nell, you—" He hesitated. I wanted for the first time to know what he was going to say. "You wouldn't—" He pulled the little velcro belt around his miniature umbrella so it became a neat baton. He held it up in his right hand and looked, somehow, like the Statue of Liberty. "I don't know," he concluded, and went inside.

JAM

BARRY NEVER EXPECTED MISHTI TO GO TO DINNER WITH HIM. HE expected you to marry him, because he is gregarious and rich and you were the opposite and old enough to crave your inverse, but he never expected Mishti, a woman too young to need anything from anyone, to want anything from him.

Mishti says he's so *worried* during their dinners he can hardly eat. She says his worry is universal. He looks at her and he can't say no to the prize he's baffled to have won, and he can't say yes to losing you, because even he knows what he has. If Barry Estlin has ever been in a tight spot, this is it. There is something awful about watching a man get what he always wanted.

Barry really loves you. Barry from his bottom thinks you are the celestial alien you are. Barry can't believe his good fortune so he tests it again and again, as if to prove his life isn't a fluke. Mishti has now given him more good fortune than he knows how to have. She's called his Midas bluff and she's the first golden mammal without a heartbeat, stiff in his hand. He knows you're next, his prize pet, soon inanimate. I see Barry's childhood dogs turning now too, golden Labrador, golden Wiener, fat Barry in a gilt room, panting, suffocating, terribly and hopelessly animate. I think Barry has always admired dogs because they are satisfied with a bone and he is never satisfied. He *wants* to be satisfied, you know. He just confuses satisfaction for boredom, every time it comes near.

Do you remember that Christmas Eve in Astoria, as you spooned

strawberry jam onto a cutting board to serve with cheese, you told
me a story about strawberry jam: You'd spent the week of Thanksgiving with Barry at his place (the way you pronounced "his place"
that night carried no trace of recognition that it would soon and
forever be yours) and you'd washed every dish the whole week,
by hand, all the Thanksgiving serving platters, everything, even
though he had a dishwasher, because you wanted to be good and
your father had taught you to love dishwashing and you'd wanted
to find some small way to express your respect for the grandeur
and polish of his house? And then, Sunday breakfast, finally relaxed, eating toast, a bit of strawberry jam fell from your knife onto
the floor. And you knew you'd wipe it up, as you knew you'd wash
all the dishes, right after breakfast, but you wanted to eat your toast
while it was hot, and there was still more jam on the knife, and you
kept spreading, then eating. Barry glared at the floor, at you, and
said, "You're not going to clean that up?"

"After I'd washed all his dishes," you told me, "after he'd let me
just wash and wash, to cast me as some kind of slob?" I hadn't responded. "This from a man who mass orders his coffee mugs, two
dozen white, two dozen black, from a hotel supplier because he
wants them to be *normal*." I hadn't seen the connection. "He's so
righteously intolerant of anything that breaks his code of order, but
he copies his code of order from hotel chains," you said, "he can't
even come up with his own rules."

He wants to be satisfied, you know. He wants to be satisfied in a
normal way. Normal as anybody, as nobody, Barry Estlin. Maybe
after Mishti is through with him he'll remember that he's always
been satisfied, and he'll like living, living the way he used to, with
you, and you'll like living the way he used to, too.

BEANS

"FROM BEHIND."

"Stop."

"What? You asked. I fuck her from behind."

We were sitting in an empty Chinese restaurant, a speaker above the door was playing a wind instrument I could hardly hear but the sound moved through my veins like a sleeping pill, I couldn't stand up and walk out and break that peace. Tom's ever longer hair swayed under the ceiling fan.

"Forget I asked. I'm sorry I asked."

"She really likes it." It was as if all my ambivalence toward him in bed were coming back in the form of a viper, as if he now had the evidence to prove his desirability, as if I'd been wrong to not want him and he'd built his case. "She keeps asking for more and more. We finish and she wants more."

"You must be very satisfying," I said, ten cold sesame noodles dangling from my lips like a car wash.

He paused. Joan I started to cry.

"What the hell, Nell," a new rhyme for him, "what?"

I didn't know what. I hated myself for never having wanted him, I didn't know what was wrong with me, I didn't want to fuck you from behind, I didn't have a pulse.

"Jesus Christ I won't tell you any more," he said, quietly, "I thought we were, you know, enlightened exes who could maintain a sexual discourse."

I wished for a moment that Tom had a sister whom I could fuck from behind and tell him about it. The closest thing was his mother, Mother Veronica, a woman so apparently cold-blooded I wished nothing more for her than that somewhere, sometimes, her husband Harvey succeeded in holding her in whatever way she privately hoped to be held. I stopped my tears by imagining Veronica and Harvey *snuggling*, a ridiculous word for Tom's mother, snuggling with all their might, under Harvey's valuable Hans Holbein the Younger.

Another man, or any woman, would have asked me just then *What are you thinking about* and I would have said *Your mother snuggling* and we would have been able to return to our noodles in good faith but Tom in those blank moments asks himself what he is thinking about.

The waiter came by and refilled our waters. Tom abruptly grasped the bowl of orange wonton crackers, threw them down his throat, and then asked the waiter to bring more of them. The waiter laughed because he's a nice guy. I slid the rest of the sesame noodles onto my plate, as if we were in a race or interested in wastelessness. The waiter brought more crackers, took the empty plate. For a moment there was nothing in the center of the table and we both looked at the brown wood.

"Do you feel any guilt?" I asked the table.

"She started it," he said. "More to the point have *you* ever felt any guilt? You've been, what, casting spells against this marriage for years. You probably have more to do with it than I do."

I rehearsed the work Mishti and I had done Halloween night. I wondered if Tom fucking Joan away from Barry counted—lemon balm, clover, ginger, High John the Conqueror, rowan, wahoo, Winter's bark—as "success."

The wood turned, as I stared at it, into an oval of string beans, chili oil, no pork, for some reason Tom the Uber Goy doesn't like pork. The beans steamed great Greek columns of steam. Tom crunched a wonton cracker and I lifted my plate to my mouth and began perversely licking the peanut sauce from it until it was clean. Then the beans were cooler and we could begin.

Tom took one, one bean, with his fingers, and put it on his plate. I did the same.

"Tell me about the *Captivity* hanging," I said, my pawn to E5.

"Well Joan was right—they're not thistles they're bistort." Somehow he had already taken my pawn. He took three more beans between two fingers and dropped them onto his plate. Then he arranged the four beans into a hash sign. I grabbed a whole handful of beans, my palm smeared with a million oils, and dropped them onto my plate like pickup sticks. I built a double hash: four on top of four, the beginning of a Jenga tower. I looked up and Tom had built his tower three stories high. I pulled a bean from the bottom of the serving plate and ate it.

He chose to use a fork for the first bean he actually ate. Tom could be so quietly and deeply critical when he disapproved, and he disapproved of such eclectic and unpredictable things, I'd always been nervous about what he judged in me and resentful that he should be able to judge with such force. The tidy mercy of a breakup is how immediately the judgments, and the fear of judgments, evaporate. I could eat with my fingers again, who cared. All I wanted to do now was build a bean tower higher than his, and I knew I could.

"Now that you've correctly identified the bordering herbs around the unicorn's feet, they have no choice but to name you a Master of Medieval and Renaissance Studies," I said. "You get your diploma when, June?"

Tom nodded and then began simply and mellifluously humming "Beauty School Dropout" at me as he stacked and stacked his beans. I looked into his eyes and wiped the red chili oil from my fingers under my right eye and my left, the most glistening, fragrant war paint. You would have leaned across the table and licked it off me. I know you would. You like living. Tom reached for his fork, the fork of civilization, and ate from the serving plate.

CASHEW

DO NOT EAT A RAW CASHEW DO NOT EAT A RAW RED KIDNEY BEAN DO
not eat elderberry or *a potato* do not eat the rind of a mango do not
put a hydrangea flower in your mouth and a daffodil will induce
severe drooling and aloe the healer will make you convulse.

Cashew shells and poison ivy are covered in the same oil, uru-
shiol, if it touches you it spreads a rash through your armpits, but-
tocks, groin. The nuts you love are fine but they've been boiled out
of their shells. To come into any contact with the uncooked shell is
to fall into the poison ivy patch at the side of the Appalachian Trail.

Kidney beans house phytohemagglutinin. The elderberry carries cyanide. The potato, uncooked and exposed to sunlight, is
loaded with solanine poison. A potato that's begun to turn green is
remorselessly, ferociously toxic.

I don't understand how it occurred to humans to cook the ined-
ible into the edible. Why we peel the mango. Why daffodils go on
the vase on the table and not the plate, why aloe is softened into a
goo, where we found as a species the courage to say this bad thing
can be made good again, can be made, furthermore, delicious!

It's religious, it's a very small, very daily resurrection.

It's a courtship of the sinister.

Whose shell would you boil off and what's the flavor of their
inner nut?

Joan have I been itching from the oil of your outsides and has
Tom made it through to your safe meat?

WAFFLES

MISHTI HAD INVITED ME TO A PANCAKE BREAKFAST WITH CARLO because she wanted me to get to know him better, but after twenty minutes Carlo hadn't yet come.

We were sitting at Sarabeth's on Amsterdam, which seemed that morning to be an odd place for anyone to sit voluntarily. It felt like crouching in the hot insides of a Macy's Parade float sponsored by Pillsbury.

Mishti needed a way to get the meal started, in Carlo's absence or to avenge Carlo's absence, so she ordered something from the "Fruity Beginnings" section of the menu that cost thirteen dollars. I realized that breakfast was on Carlo. The empty floral-upholstered chair became at once the most substantial presence at the table.

I leaned back into my own upholstery in silence because I wanted to tell Mishti about you and Tom and I couldn't. What confused me most was that I didn't know how she'd respond. Would it mainly surprise her that Tom *did* something? The funny little verbs for fucking filled me like zoo animals: *did, banged, boned*—would she protest the grading advantage? Would she laugh at Barry? Would she marry Barry herself?

I wondered if she could hear my thoughts (or indeed if she had always been able to hear my thoughts, if our friendship had been founded on that kind of channel) when she volunteered, "The thing that makes it easy is that Barry will never actually leave Joan. And

Joan's too deep in the logistics of Barry's financial life to leave him, either."

I was grateful for my previous silence then because it wasn't weird to stay silent, to betray nothing on my face. Carlo rushed in.

"Mendelson," he said, as he took his seat. "Mendelson," he repeated.

Mishti had just finished her berry bowl and she glared at Carlo while licking the curve of her spoon. Carlo had apparently exerted himself—a thin mist of sweat, the most sweat I could imagine his body embarrassing itself by producing, mustached his upper lip. He knew it was there and he wiped it.

"He needs me, day and night, and I can't find a way to say no to him."

The bafflement about Carlo was that he really was excellent, his excellence was pristine, and he was sexy too, and the fact that I didn't appreciate him was my fault.

He ordered a lemon ricotta waffle and it came instantly, as if a certain number of lemon ricotta waffles were ordered each morning and they had them ready to deploy. Mishti and I had both ordered omelets that came out a minute afterward.

"Tell Nell about Bermuda," Carlo cut his waffle along its grid lines, "did you tell her about Bermuda? Mishti and I are going to Bermuda."

"For Christmas," said Mishti, dutifully, as if she hadn't already told me. She didn't touch the eggs in front of her, she wanted to watch our interaction closely, she wanted to ensure its success.

"I've heard."

Carlo reached out across the table and took Mishti's hand. He smiled so wide it was actually beautiful and luminous. He couldn't wait to go to Bermuda with Mishti. He looked at her with eyes that said *You're hot and smart* and he looked at me and said that he loved dolphins, and that there's supposed to be an incredible aquarium.

"I want you to put all the textbooks away and relax," he told her, holding her hand. "It's going to be our real vacation."

Mishti smiled a sincere and bashful smile because she has never been encouraged to relax in her entire overachieving life and finals are coming up and the truth is she's exhausted.

We ate in silence for a little while then. Carlo finished his waffle. He broke the silence to say he loved it. "Great fucking waffle." I finished my omelet and loved it too, but I never don't love an egg, no matter what you do to it. "Love a motherfucking omelet!" I offered, to be a good sport, but then I felt very shy and sorry, and started thinking about Tom's mother and my fucking his imaginary sister. Mishti didn't eat. I wished she would take a bite but she was trying to think of something to say, something that would open Carlo up and reveal him to me.

I, in counter-loyalty, wanted Carlo to see that Mishti would never fully reveal *herself* to *him*, that the reflection of himself he saw in her was the excellent surface of a pool, a pool whose floor was irregular and too deep to see.

"Well, Joan's distracted too," I said, to remind him that he had been late, that Mishti and I talked about things he didn't know.

Mishti straightened her neck and said, "You're kidding." I wasn't sure how much she had understood. She looked over my head at nothing, as if looking out a window, and seemed overtaken by total disgust—I hadn't included disgust as one of the reaction options, but Mishti no longer seemed to be breathing in or out.

A waiter passed behind our table and Carlo spun around and stopped him and asked for the check, simultaneously handing over his credit card. During the exchange Mishti whispered to me, "Who?" and I shrugged and told her, "Tom," as if it weren't a very big deal.

"But she's . . ." Mishti was struggling with something I couldn't identify. "But she's so *old*," Mishti concluded, a little too loudly. Carlo turned back around and faced us. Mishti kept talking: "Why would *she* be the one he wants?"

I hadn't expected this particular grievance. I thought Mishti would mock you for cradle robbing, or mock Tom for ladder climbing, or mock sexual intercourse itself for being such a pathetic human activity, but she seemed utterly and specifically disappointed that Tom had chosen you. I'd never known Tom's choices to matter to her at all, one way or another. Her disappointment gave your fucking a legitimacy I hadn't previously given it.

She said, "The Joan epidemic! It was bad enough coming from you—you had to teach it to Tom? What's wrong with *both of you*?"

I said, "Sloppy Cupid?"

Carlo's phone, which had been lying face up beside his water glass, began to buzz and Barry's pumpkin face filled up the screen. BARRY, it buzzed, BARRY. BARRY.

My eyes shot up at Mishti stupidly, instinctively, my very pupils repeating BARRY, BARRY at her.

Mishti gathered her entire soul in the pit of her stomach, I watched every light retreat from her eyes and relocate, she became a tough piece of rock inside herself and her flesh became irrelevant. She had nothing to hide. She hid herself. She squinted and looked like a superhero.

"Babe," Carlo said to her, "Babe listen I gotta go."

HONEY

SHE TOLD BARRY TO PUT IT BETWEEN HER BREASTS.

She felt its weight thunk down.

She wanted his heat.

He gave her his finger.

He denied her his fist.

He wanted her heaven.

She wanted it to take her whole body up.

She wanted to take everything.

She told him harder.

He tried.

He could make her come sometimes and sometimes he couldn't wait.

He gave her everything.

She wanted control.

She took control.

She opened completely.

She took everything.

She told me it never hurt.

She told me he could be crazy tender.

YOGURT

I STOOD BEHIND THE BAR POURING AN OLD MAN A LONG JACK AND
thinking about everyone doing each other, everyone getting it
done, doing, done, and what could I do, I'd over-frozen my monkshood seeds and my castor hadn't bloomed. I couldn't buy any more
seeds, I needed to use my next shifts to pay Tom back for lunch and
probably other things, years of miscellaneous expenses I couldn't
remember, I suddenly wanted to clear my accounts with him, to
clear myself of him, and to get my own groceries. I pretend I don't
need groceries but I'm going to develop early-onset cataracts for
lack of protein. When I imagine winning the lottery now I imagine
Greek yogurt: for life! I don't even want a flavor. I want so much
full-fat original Fage that I could swim laps in it.

One thing you wouldn't expect is that you can use Greek yogurt
as a sauce for tortellini. I'd even call it the best of all possible sauces.

Joan I'm not getting anywhere. Joan you probably hate Greek
yogurt, it probably isn't even really Greek. Joan why are you sleeping with Tom? Why are you a living creature who needs to sleep at
all? How am I supposed to sleep when I have such a library of hei-
nous imagery to project for myself on my eyelids? In every eyelid
movie Tom's long hair is brushing gray paint up the length of your
back. I get up from the floor and squint at my flowerpots. I've
planted my stupid frozen monkshood but everyone will tell you
they're touchy the first year ("finicky about germination!" "don't
expect them all to germinate!" "don't panic!" "dammit!") and my

hopes are low. They could grow to be four feet tall if they grew and blossomed, and so much blue would be a richness, but I need their roots most of all and if they don't send out roots this year, they don't.

I'm betting on the castor. The first tiny seedlings have come up from one of the two seeds, can you believe it, you screwed my ex-boyfriend but I got a castor plant to grow in December. These so-called ornamental breeds throw up seedlings in one to three weeks and mine, because they are mine, took five weeks but I'll take it. We are all very good at taking.

I just want to show that it's possible to stop something from happening. I know I didn't stop you and Tom from happening. I— I want to show that anything can change its course. To reset something's destination from *this* to *that*, such that even when it's at *this*, it isn't there yet. The aconite and the ricin are already here in my apartment doing what they think they're built to do, being bad, and I'm trying to teach them that they have other options. They could become architects. Schoolteachers. They're city kids but they could live in the country if they wanted to. They'd learn how. They'd start hiking. On the weekends they'd churn butter.

If ricin is defined by its toxicity, what will define a nontoxic or detoxified ricin? It gets to be a whole new soul. It gets to like living. Joan I don't blame you for changing your destination. But even you, right now, in the height of your abandon, can't think of Tom as *there*.

NUTS

YOUR EMAIL SAID THE GRANT WOULD COVER SIX MONTHS OF RE-
search with some drool-bait adverb like "generously" or "comfort-
ably." I deleted it and then permanently deleted it like a deranged
person because I was reading it too many times.

I guess it's a relief that the National Science Foundation also
finds you worthy of recognition. Mishti had started to convince me
that my admiration was misplaced; it isn't misplaced. You are
63,446 dollars good, Award #1808234, Original Start Date: December 15, Projected Duration: 6 months. The funding council unani-
mously wagers that your pollen-pistil work is going to help out our
country's bees.

We met on the steps of the library because it was snowing and
you wanted to be snowed on. You were completely bundled, black
hat, black scarf, black gloves, black boots, but rising up toward your
jaw, out from under the top of your scarf, I saw, very purple, a
hickey.

A hickey, Joan.

You *wanted to be snowed on.*

The first time you allowed your eyes to meet my eyes you
looked like a woman in love. You, too, are a deranged person.
You looked at me with a peaked, frantic, paranoid flush as if the
snowflakes could hear us, as if your dry skin had turned into a tarp
of secrets.

The first thing you wanted to know was how often Mishti saw Barry. There was something darkly enlightened about the way your husband's infidelity wounded you not at all, and only gave you the thrilling gift of your own previously inconceivable infidelity. I told you once a week, though I no longer knew if that was true. "Good," you said, "good, but let's ramp it up a little," and I told you to get a goddamn grip.

"What?"

"Isn't there some orderly way to do this?" I said, pathetically. "Do what?" you said. "Destroy yourself." You laughed. "I just want a little more time with him."

"So actually exit your marriage."

"I don't want *that* much time with him."

"Gross."

"Toward Tom I feel only, but pure, lust."

"I don't think that's what Mishti is feeling."

"I can't imagine what Mishti is feeling," you said, "Barry's revolting."

I looked at you then as if you had been lying to me for five years, which you had.

You felt the very hot wrath in me and burst into an enormous smile, the biggest I'd ever seen grace your face, and you said, "I can hire an assistant, Nell."

"What."

"I'm eligible for up to twenty-five thousand additional dollars if I hire an assistant from the university system *to assist in expanding my study.*"

"Between your student boyfriend and your husband's student girlfriend, I'd say you have two excellent, expansive candidates."

"I'm having good sex, Nell. And I want to hire you. What do you want?"

You looked at me and I felt I'd been in an accident, that you were asking me to remember my date of birth.

"I want to bind aconite alkaloids to flecainide acetate, so they cancel each other out."

"Great," you said. "Let's go."

You stood up then and started walking down the steps, I had no idea where you were going and the steps were slippery and I hate falling down and I am starting to think I hate you. I chased after you as if you were my mother.

"Joan, hey, what are you talking about," I called forward through the matrix of snowflakes that separated us, I caught up to you, "what does *let's go* mean here?"

"You tell me, what do you need? A monkshood starter?"

I didn't want to tell you that I'd forgotten my seeds in the freezer, that I'd over-corrected their dormancy and that they were almost certain to fail. So I said I needed a steady acetate supply, which was also true, and probably a better use of the foundation's money anyway, as flecainide is way more expensive than seeds. "And taspine resin," I threw in, for good measure, remembering Mishti's expensive sample. I got my first flashing sense of the shopping list I could actually assemble. I didn't trust it, I didn't trust it to be possible, or mine.

"Great," you kept walking, "so the second the assistant allowance comes in I'll register you and you can go nuts. I'm happy," you said, "because it's really about time you went nuts." I think you were trading me my work for my boyfriend. It was a trade I was willing to make.

I stopped, I had nothing more to say and nowhere to go, and you just kept walking, walking forward, aimless and totally confident, as if the entire frozen and sparkling world were a private lounge built exclusively for people who have good sex.

FISH

WHEN WE FIRST MET, I DIDN'T WANT YOU. I DIDN'T WANT TO TOUCH you! I didn't want to wrap my jiggly arms around you, I didn't want to leave a hickey on your very long neck. These things moreover wouldn't have occurred to me; sex hadn't much existed in Kansas and where it did exist it appeared reserved for boy and girl varsity athletes. I'd never wanted what those kids had, spit and ponytails, and I'd never imagined my own alternatives. Instead I did my homework. I found my privacy, my sensuality, by plunging my feet into pond muck. Scattering schools of invisible fish.

I met you and I didn't want you. Why want you? I'd never seen a grown woman wanted. I'd seen my father reach into the sink drain and remove wet slices of onion, because my mother couldn't suffer their texture. That was enough devotion. I wanted an A, an adviser, a witness to my tiny genius. I wanted a mother more esoteric and *contemporary* than my own. I wanted a relation more rigorous than friendship. I wanted partnership. I wanted science.

It surprised me when I loved your shoulders. Your body surprised me. Who could have expected your freckles, your freckles on your shoulders? It surprised me when the flatness of your chest looked to me like a topographical map of Kansas, and when, on certain winter nights, as the city turned unbearably loud and bleary, I thought it might be comfortable to go back and live there, on top of you. It surprised me when your first short-sleeved shirt of spring contracted my abdomen. It surprised me when, on certain summer nights, as the city teemed with humidity and odor, I thought it might be pleasant to be one layer of uncolored nail polish lying in rest over your fingernails.

I still wanted everything I'd wanted before—your agreement, your affirmation, your success that could illuminate and create my own—but now I also wanted your waist, some way of cupping the sides of your waist with my wrinkly creased palms, and your earlobes, some way of knowing their taste. At first I called these additional desires *par for the course*. I grouped them into my reverence. I wrote them off as side effects of my ambition. I congratulated myself for going whole hog. There was no danger; I knew you could never want me. My daydreams, my nightdreams were my own. What else could I call my own?

Then one afternoon, my third year, you were making a joke about Barry. You and he had recently celebrated your paper anniversary and it had been appropriately, this was your word, *dry*. I asked you what you meant. We were standing in the women's room of Butler Library, on our way to a research techniques symposium. You'd just finished washing your hands. You reached your left hand, full of rings, to my face and wiped the water off on my cheek. Your hand pulled down smooth and hard until your fingers dropped from my chin.

"No *glide*," you said.

As if I could speak.

You were laughing because you found your own sexual dissatisfaction funny and because you felt comfortable around me. Your laughter made me feel comfortable around myself, an insane luxury. You were in a punchy, pre-symposium mood, the mood you always enter when you know you're about to be bored. You wiped your other hand off on my forearm and it rushed to my elbow as if down a Slip 'n Slide.

"You've got nice skin," you said, "easy."

You were already leaving the room and I watched you push open the swinging door and I thought, I had the unbelievable notion: you wanted me. Which meant, which opened up, which permitted: I wanted you something terrible.

Maybe cowards can only desire when they feel desired. Maybe runts need encouragement. Maybe my central identity is coward runt. In any case, you introduced a crazy and immense idea to me that day.

You've never touched me since. It has become increasingly shocking that you ever did. You are self-possessed, but not reckless. You behave. My confidence has become more circumscribed, maybe more accurate. I think you were simply tired of yourself, that day, washing your hands in the library bathroom, tired of yourself and your Barry, so you took interest in me, the most available *other*.

I know, you didn't really want me. You wanted the otherness.

Me, I still want you something terrible.

LAMB

TOM SAYS YOUR FINAL WAS *HARD*. HE DIDN'T STUDY BECAUSE HE didn't think he needed to. That makes him an idiot. The number one thing to know about you is that you require *further study*. Tom completely missed the point. Fucking you counts for nothing, I keep telling myself, although it apparently makes your day. I hope he fails your final, as he deserves to, and that his heart breaks. No, it isn't that vindictive. I hope our hearts break.

I told Tom I wanted to give him back some money and he found that vulgar and annoying and told me to meet him at the Cloisters, as if its grace could heal and correct me.

The fortress stood at the top of Fort Tryon Park like a taxidermy grizzly bear, dead and large and hard. But when I entered its arched doorway its grace did heal and correct me. I'd walked up the long and dreary Margaret Corbin Drive with my hood up to the cold, I'd forgotten my headphones and entertained myself by pretending to be a dismal monk, kicking fallen yellow oak leaves that hadn't yet disintegrated and admiring how long the autumn had lasted, how the cold hadn't ruined anything. The river waited to my left like a sleeping fish, silvery and languageless, coughing up the great banks of the Palisades without any effort. A tanker stood still on its surface, crazily heavy, reminding me that I was a twig who could walk. I walked and walked, up the shoulder while cars swerved around me—there's no clear delineation between where people should

walk and where cars should drive on the road to the Cloisters because it's a singular and pure approach to an old place.

I climbed the fake-ancient and certainly cursed stairs to the
front gate. It surprised me to find electric lights installed along
the entrance corridor. They'd been tinted yellow to imitate age, but
the columns they lit up signified age of a different order. I wanted
to loiter in the dark with all the old stone and to turn into stone
myself. I knew Tom was waiting inside, hot and human and growing hair. I took my hood down and checked my coat.

There he stood, by the Romanesque fountain of a lion drooling
into a tub. The sound it made was utterly peaceful, individual drops
on marble, the expression of the lion's face lunatic and hilarious.
Tom, because he likes living, stood smiling at the hilarious lion.
When he heard me approach, he offered the same smile to me.

"Pilgrim," he said.

"Lordship."

If I acquiesced to Tom's ego and turf here, he'd let me out
quickly; I'd drop the money into his coat pocket (evidently also
checked, he stood in a thin henley the gray of his eyes) and I'd walk
off in an easy way, in fact walking out of his life: quietly, finally.

We circled the Cuxa Cloister, Catalan, year 1130, an arcade of
columns whose capitals showed conjoined lions eating men. The
monastery had been sacked in the seventeenth century, fell into
ruin by the nineteenth, and had been reconstructed here at a quar-
ter its original size. It was still huge, commanding. Above us the
Lamb of God danced on the head of a cherub, and the cherub
folded two of his four wings over his chest as a private blanket.

Tom walked, elegantly ogling each object so I'd understand
him to be an attentive person. We stopped before twin basins, the

Lavabo, from the Latin for "I will wash." *I will wash*, I promised myself, having lapsed, having become a little pillar of body oil. I wished I could pull my hood up again and cover my neglected scalp but I wanted to disgust Tom a little, I wanted to get my grease on him. Tom's hair was clean and sheeny. Sometimes he touched it, as if to get back in touch with himself. Sometimes even I wanted to touch it. I looked forward to the day that touching Tom's hair would cease to be an option for me—that day became tomorrow. We shared too much, we wanted too little from each other. I wanted a clean break from him, or at least a break of any kind.

"She's a real adult," Tom said, as if we'd been talking about you, and I thought I would suffer more XXX annals. "She confirms the fact that I'm a child."

I thought of Mishti saying, "She's so . . . *old*." I wondered what Tom found arousing—it hadn't been me, and it hadn't been any of the countless Miss America contestants who'd solicited him throughout college. I looked at his body grown high, his hair grown long, the fuzz on the backs of his hands, the bone in his jaw, the bulge in his neck, and told him, "You aren't childish."

"I think if the moment came, and somebody said, *Tom*, do something, say something, be something, believe something, if I became, you know, needed—needed in some urgent way to, you know, *deliver*," he clawed his right fingernails into his left index finger, turning the knuckle white, "I'd fudge." He let the finger go. "I worry I'm a serial fudger."

Against everything I knew of Tom's inconstancies, his cowardice, and the pulsing envy I felt for his scratched and pinkened finger that had stroked yours, I placed my hand across one of his large flat shoulder blades and said, "You're the genuine article."

Tom laughed because he wants so badly to be genuine.

"Everybody's a fake in some way," he said. "You know? Well, everybody except Mishti."

"Mishti wears platform boots for fake height, and eyebrow paint for fake impact, and padded bras."

"Yeah, but she's only about what she's about. She owns it. She isn't pretending anything, and she does—she has—exactly what she wants. She actually . . . shines."

"That's true, shining is her goal."

"I don't know why she puts up with you, you're so not shiny."

"Why did you put up with me?"

"I'd be her sidekick, but she finds my presence preposterous."

"Your presence is preposterous."

A chamber off the cloister's main courtyard described itself as a place to discuss, consider, and observe the Rule of Saint Benedict, a code of monastic behavior that taught monks how to live right. We walked past it as if we could never ever live right. I wanted to turn back and sit there as much as I wanted you. I looked at Tom and filled up with jealous exhaustion. Preposterous or not, he had landed in the promised land. He kept walking straight past the monks' educational courtyard. Maybe Tom, being the one who holds your hand, doesn't need any instruction. His life cannot be improved.

The copper alloy *Refectory Bell* on the next wall had been inscribed:

TINNIO PRANSVRIS CENATVRIS BIBITVRIS

"I RING FOR BREAKFAST, DRINKS, AND DINNER"

I looked at the bell thinking *No one would answer me,* and Tom looked at the bell thinking *I should get myself a bell.* In the accompanying *Glossarium* illustration two long-haired and timeless men-women wearing patterned gowns rang bells at each other, grinning as if to say *Breakfast.* Tom and I wanted to say something to each other about the innumerable and miserable coffee mornings we'd spent together fudging but nothing came and we entered the shadow of an enormous camel.

The camel hung opposite a dragon in a vaulted hall. The dragon, brave and cartoonish enough to be a Picasso, had been frescoed around 1200 for the "aesthetic delight" of a Benedictine monastery. We turned a corner into a more austere room where one limestone fragment hung high on a wall, far overhead, with a sign at eye level that read only:

Angel.

Tom walked from hall to hall as if he'd grown up here in a back bedchamber. He led me directly to a statue of *Christ Child with an Apple* whose butt had been painted gum pink. Above the child, the warrior-archangel Michael was treading on a fleshy dragon. The description called the dragon "a symbol of the devil" and for a moment I faltered, full of my own solitude and regret, mourning the hideous sacrifice of Rachel Simons, affiliating myself with the devil. Then I tried to affiliate myself with the cartoon, I tried to christen myself Pablo, I tried to walk backwards into the Benedictine schoolroom. Tom walked ahead into his own destination, the tapestry room, which he'd apparently saved for last. He turned over his shoulder to see if I would follow. I followed, Joan, I understand. He is not losing his power, you are not losing your mind. I am not losing you.

The *Unicorn in Captivity* towered over Tom, plainly and unmistakably his master. I left him alone and looked at the hanging to his right: *The Unicorn Is Found*. All about the unicorn's tail scrambled dogs and rabbits. Men assembled at the top of the tapestry like a jury. I read the men's faces from left to right, there were twelve of them, and all of them were Tom. They wore ringlets and fine garments, their faces had all been cut from the same moon-colored marble, their features smooth and dignified, their limbs long, their pride immeasurable. The unicorn dips its horn into a pool of water falling from a lion's mouth, the same kind of fountain that made such a good noise with its water, earlier, in a cloister that now felt imaginary.

"You could be a real adult if you wanted to be," I said, because other people's self-loathing is the only thing that makes me confident. "You are capable." He lifted his phone and took a couple pictures of the walls. I wanted him to call me your only partner. I wanted him to resign.

"I suppose," he said, vague and bored. I'd extended the conversation past his interest and now my speaking was disturbing his unicorn time. I walked away from Tom and down a flight of stairs.

Saint Fiacre, of alabaster, stood on a pedestal, his eyes closed. "Holding a shovel in one hand, Saint Fiacre is presented as the patron saint of gardeners," I read first, then, "particularly renowned for curing hemorrhoids." I pictured the pink butt of the Christ Child. Fiacre, in his comparative solemnity, was a colorless yellow.

His head fell against his own shoulder in the most patient melancholy. I stood and genuinely worshipped Saint Fiacre. I wanted some air. I found an exit that led me, as if by his guidance, into an herb garden exhibiting over two hundred medieval plants. Outside it felt less like winter than the lack of every season: a harsh, open, blank day that had never been colored in. All the same it was freezing and for the thousandth time I missed my coat. I missed the way my hood had held my head and taken care of it. I don't miss my parents *per se* but I do miss care. Joan if you ever let me care for you I will ask for nothing in return, and you will occasionally shield me in some essentially warm way that induces my deepest gratitude. I made a slow lap of the plant beds, depositing my little dragon puff of breath above each sign:

Horseheal, Peony, Feverfew, Asparagus.

Figwort, Sneezewort, and Self-Heal.

Horned Poppy and Mole Plant.

Mouse-Ear Hawkweed.

Squirting Cucumber.

Common Valerian, Annual Sage, Birthwort, Bearded Iris.

Madder, Weld.

Lady's Bedstraw, Dyer's Alkanet.

Flax, Woad, Agrimony.

Bugle, and a full rush of Aconite Monkshood.

In one bunch, at the base of a gnarled tree: Quince, Cowslip, and Christmas Rose—Black Hellebore.

Hound's-Tongue. Bistort. Adderwort, next to Dragon Arum.

Tom hadn't yet found or followed me, none of the museum's visitors would leave the heated building, I stood alone with my favorite creatures. Tom stood alone with his favorite creatures. There's a version of the world in which there's room for all of us. In which we all belong here, also anywhere, even everywhere. Who did you stand with, that cold day, your lover and your servant in their rightful places, your rightful place nowhere?

Your email popped up on his phone as we were standing in the coat check line. He swiped it open immediately and didn't stop me from blatantly hunching over to read along. Leaning against him to see the screen was the most physical contact we'd had since the last time we'd slept together. He sleeps with someone better now, I thought. I sleep on the floor with a bag of dirt. Rightful places. The department's Thanksgiving party had been so weird, you wrote, you wanted to throw a better Christmas party, at your home. The email was addressed to all five of us, and it was ludicrous to see our names together in a row. I pictured you asking Barry for Carlo's email address and the multiple simultaneous panic attacks that must have provoked through the citywide energy net.

Tom blanched. "What does Joan want from me?" was the odd thing he said.

"From *you*?"

"I have to monkey myself in front of her husband like a monkey?"

"I think that's a small price to pay."

"Who's paying? What a fucking circus."

I saw the six of us seated around a ping-pong table under the high center of a tent. You and I would sit at the table ends like monarchs. The email said Sunday at seven o'clock. I mutely postponed walking out of Tom's life to Monday.

A woman handed us our two coats, they'd been nuzzling each other on adjacent hangers, and I tipped her with the six cash dollars I had from tips crumpled in my jeans pocket, showing Tom that I could afford generosity. He didn't register the exchange at all, he was rereading your email, scowling at it, as if it were a draft notice. I had no remaining sympathy for him in what I'm sure he dubbed his *predicament*, and having repaid him a miscellaneous and insufficient but satisfying $150, I readied myself for your party, knowing I'd be the only guest with nothing to lose and everything to eat.

BERRY

I CARRIED A BOUQUET FOR THE HOSTESS. YOU OPENED THE DOOR
wearing a floor-length charcoal nightgown. You'd let your braid
out and your crimped hair wreathed your shoulders. Your twin
stone earrings hung like upended monoliths from each lobe. You
had painted your fingernails white. You had darkened your eye-
lashes and eyelids and eyebrows. Your nightgown was strangely
formal and acceptable. You had opened the gown's top button to
reveal your collarbone. A tiny moonstone shuddered on its chain in
the collarbone's middle hollow. I thought in all plainness that I
would now expressly die. You reached your arms out toward me
and pulled one sleeve of my coat off my arm, I gave the bouquet to
my other hand, you pulled off the other sleeve, and with the down
corpse of my soul in your arms you receded into the darkness of
your comfortable home.

The dangling string of the coat closet's ceiling light kept touching, touching your ear as if whispering formulas for the speed of
light into you, you didn't hush it or flick it away, you hung up my
coat, you took a long time of it, I waited for you right there in the
underlit foyer. When you finally pulled the string and closed the
door and turned around the foyer fell even darker and you seemed
surprised by my flowers, as if you hadn't seen them in the hall, as if
you'd also been too busy dying out there. I took this as unbelievable
flattery. I held the bouquet out to you proudly, in absolute obedi-
ence. You didn't take it or speak or move. You wanted a prelude.

"Tulip," I said, pointing to the single pink bulb, "for triumph over yourself."

"And?" you said. What a remarkable invitation. And the rest of my life, I could wrap in paper and give you, and the largest smell of the smallest leaf of basil, and a cardinal's breast feathers, and a pack of Junior Mints, and a wall of spontaneous ivy.

"Marsh mallow," I said, pointing to the fluffy beard beneath the tulip, "because it produces a polysaccharide solution that resembles human mucus and this snot can be used as a gargle or an eyewash."

Nothing.

"Rosemary, so you don't forget. Shepherd's purse, for a blood coagulant. Dandelion, for a blood thinner. Wintergreen, for flatulence. Skullcap, for restlessness. Tansy, for hysteria. Valerian, also for hysteria. Elder for the part-festive part-toxic red berries. All swathed in lily of the valley, for *marital happiness*."

Once again you reached your arms out toward me and this time you filled both your hands with my lilies. You went around the perimeter of the bouquet grabbing the white blossoms everywhere they appeared and yanked them out of the bouquet as if from a tiger's teeth and hurled them onto the ground. You looked at me as if you would kill me and said, "Lilies killed my cat." Then I started laughing so hard I couldn't stop. You took the rest of the stalks from my shaking hands and spun to the kitchen to put them somewhere and left me where I shook and left the lilies on the floor and Amanda came lumbering over to sniff them.

It looked like a bird had been eaten by a bigger bird. Red pearls interrupted the white where elderberries fell from your vigorous yanking. Amanda pushed her snout against the pile of it. I had never met Amanda before: she is a handsome, long-legged beast and I was admiring her brick coat in a daze when her tongue emerged, headed for the fattest berry. I tackled the dog. The dog found me incomprehensible. I lay with my head on the mound of tiny lilies, my arms clasped around the dog's gut. Then, as angels who fall into swamps push slowly, dumbly forward, Amanda resumed her journey, dragging me, me in my soft butt-hushing pants, smooth over the glazed wooden floor a few steps into the kitchen.

I stood up and thanked the dog and looked around your kitchen and thought, Do I deserve this. Do I deserve a dishwasher. Do I deserve a wooden door to hide the metal refrigerator door. Do I deserve a state-of-the-art metal refrigerator. Do I deserve two state-of-the-art metal refrigerators, side by side. Do I deserve a soap dish with no residue in or under it. Do I deserve a pantry.

Wealth is wasted on me, I resolved, because I don't like sushi. The best way to spend money is on sushi.

With a blue vase squeezed in the crook of your elbow you twisted an ice tray away from itself at the corners until the cubes popped up like wee English muffins from an arctic toaster. You threw them one at a time into the bottom of the vase as Mishti and I had thrown our peach wedges on Halloween. Then you filled the cold belly with water and the ice cracked and the flowers genuflected. You know the best way to do anything. I know the best way to do nothing. Your dog doesn't *do* your dog *is*. She lives her days one evolutionary intelligence ahead of us.

"Sad, Konstantinos," I said, although Konstantinos had died four years ago and I had joined you in mourning him then. Strange that I hadn't thought then of the lilies, of course it had been the lilies, the lily on your bedside windowsill, its petals inducing feline kidney failure. I have, since that Christmas, assumed you loved lilies because it was the only plant I saw in your home. I have never interrogated it because you loved it. How is it that neither of us knew about them, about what they can do to cats? As if what we love can't hurt?

You placed the vase on the windowsill behind the sink. You wiped your hands on a tea towel. The kitchen had been painted the butter color of better homes and the gilt fixtures shone a pee-tinted light. You looked at me with an enraged, apologetic expression that seemed to blame me for the yellowness, for the fact that we were getting yellow.

I met you the year you became Mrs. Estlin and you see in my face a portal back to the moment you made your choice. I met you after you were accomplished and before you were comfortable, which is any spirit's most vibrant point. I met you at your height. I watched you choose to pour cement over the then ceilingless room of your life and call it a ceiling. I watched you hang a chandelier. Every time the breeze ripples the crystals you're frightened. Every time you're frightened I'm in love with you.

You stood by the sink, watching me watch your decline into establishment and you wanted to climb me out of yourself, climb me like a painter's ladder. You can put your feet on my flat rungs, I want you to, I'm good for that use and no other, I'm firmly planted in the muck, myself. And there you stand in your long gray cosmos. I look at you and I see how absolutely each person is afflicted, regardless of station, by envy. How envy is the best distraction from the completeness of our own lives. How longing is sacred and envy is rotten longing. How hard we are on our own happiness and how generous we are toward just about anyone else, how willing we are to believe that anyone else knows how.

We couldn't find a thing to say to each other in the golden kitchen and I wanted to write you a benediction on appetite, our enormous animal appetite, and how pure appetite doesn't differentiate between nourishment and harm. About female patience and the wastefulness of wanting what others wish they didn't have. About the incredible courage and elegance of children who have not yet named their own fears. About how long we are children. About the person to whom you promise and then take back your life. That we should be capable as organisms to love and then to leave, to pledge and then repledge, is our most hopeful and cruel power.

"I'll keep the elder away from Amanda," I said.

"She's a good girl," you said.

At this point the evening fractured into distinct, miniature evenings, one after another, as if it weren't a night we were spending together but an age, an eon.

BEER

TALL, THIN, AND ALABASTER, TOM OTTAWAY OPENED THE WOOD-covered metal fridge door and took himself a beer. He carried a kind of immaculate energy around him and I wanted to take his picture, but as with the curtain I couldn't. I don't wish Tom to fade any more than I wish cliffs to crumble. You reacted electrically to the combination of me and you and him contained in the neutral kitchen, a compound unrepeated since the cheese table, and you jolted to attention with a swish of your atypically loose hair, the waves flew round and gathered on one shoulder. With this imitation of your single braid armor in place you ventured: "Who came before Nell?"

"What?" said Tom, unimaginatively.

It startled me that you'd throw such a bedsheet over our pet elephant and bring its shape into sight, call it Elephant, serve it to us hot, but it didn't surprise me.

You held an arm out toward me as if I were a piece of evidence. Then you raised your other palm to your own chest, covering that little moonstone. "Joan, preceded by Nell, preceded by whom," you pronounced clearly, I had never heard you say your own name, and I felt all at once that you had read this notebook, that you imitated my invocations. I also knew you hadn't, and I wanted you to, I wanted to give you these bodega books full of worship, bound up in mulberry branches. I wanted to hear you read yourself as I've composed you and so fulfill ourselves.

"Nobody," said Tom.

You said, "You're joking."

Tom didn't mind, he said "What?" again, and then, "I made some gross love in dorm rooms like anyone but Nell was my first *relationship*, as it were."

As it were, I knew this, I had never given it much thought. Tom had never belonged to me any more than he'd belonged to himself; his big insufferable beauty had disembodied him and this disembodied, suffering beauty had visited me for a time. That the visit had been protracted over a period of years qualified it, I suppose, as a relationship, but I wouldn't call it union, communion, or love.

"Which poor chap lost out to Barry?"

Tom had fallen into the Britishisms of our shorthand and his childhood, which meant Tom had fallen down.

"I shudder to think," he added, at which I watched you lose your patience.

"Ragnar Hjort Erlingsen," you said, as if translating Go Fuck Yourself into its ancient original language. "Youngest ever Danish parliament member. Blond, ruthless, great dancer, and real efficient."

I stood there smiling because a nobleman named Ragnar had licked the brackish Baltic Sea off your thighs and I am so perfectly wrong for you that maybe life will let me off this hook: dark, full of ruth, clumsy, comically inept. That you would choose a Barry over a Ragnar confirmed desire's basic irrelevance, relieved me of taking my irrelevant desire seriously. I could retire now, retire the heart.

Tom only then found the bottle opener in one of your gilt kitchen's six hundred drawers and cracked open his beer as violently as he could and let the discarded cap lie on the floor. You and

I looked at it and thought about strawberry jam. I picked it up because I have no dignity. Tom looked at Mishti, who'd just walked in, we hadn't even heard the doorbell, evidently Barry had.

"It's nice to see you," Tom told Mishti. Mishti sort of literally stopped in her tracks. She looked at Tom for a second as if he were mocking her. Tom's face didn't change. Mishti said, "It is?"

Tom said, "Your face is a comfort to me, here in the war zone."

You said, "What war zone?"

Tom said, "Why the interrogation?"

Mishti said, "My face is a comfort to you?"

You jumped right in and told Mishti to describe her ex. She and Tom snapped out of the eye contact gridlock they'd screeched into, and both of them focused on you. You had turned our discomfort into a parlor game. Bizarrely, Mishti and I were both wearing black turtlenecks and black jeans. It looked as though we'd planned it but I'd never seen Mishti wear black before. Carlo came in right behind her. It seemed insane that Mishti still pretended to date him, until Carlo raised his elbow slightly to shake Tom's hand and there in the little window of Carlo's armpit appeared Barry. At once they seemed to require each other, Carlo and Barry, each absurd and together amounting to 180 degrees.

"Sulky," Mishti said, game. "Hot, sulky, and idiotic."

Tom burped. "You expel idiots," he said.

"Insensitive verb choice," you said, pretending to be my friend.

I tossed the beer cap into the far trash can and made the shot but nobody saw.

"I used to think idiots were hot," said Mishti.

"They *are* hot," Tom said, for a reason I couldn't imagine.

"They're vain," said Mishti.

Tom went back to his open beer. It felt as if Tom and Mishti had been spending time together without me, that their rapport had evolved, and I remembered with a neat punch to the spleen that I really had been expelled.

"And yours?" You welcomed Carlo magnanimously, with a shocking toothy celebrity smile, and I wanted him to bow to you. I couldn't understand why no one was kissing the hem of your night-gown.

"Socialite lamp designer," he said. "She was so enamored of her own chores."

"How so?" said Tom, who had never done chores.

"Oh you know *Sometimes I make coffee at five p.m. sometimes I don't put my socks in the dryer just so I can hang them from doorknobs isn't that weird sometimes I just need a pineapple—*"

"Those are chores?" said Joan, who had always done chores.

"Eccentricities?" Carlo modified. "And to a certain extent, in moderation, of course, everyone loves eccentricities, they lubricate life. But I thought it'd be in better taste if she'd cool it a little."

"Huh," said Mishti, who was nothing if not cooled.

"So that's *my* dark past," Carlo told her. "Not so dark. We had a bazillion lamps."

How willing we were to fill in our blanks, willing and even giddy. The lamp designer, then the chemist. Or the chemist, after the lamp designer. In a more platonic course of life we would be able to love one love at a time, in sequence, without recurrence, relapse, nostalgia, or overlap. But the ones we abandon are always burning holes in the one we choose.

I pictured my utilitarian lamp standing tall and blank in Red

Hook. I pictured handing it an elaborate hat. I pictured my lamp throwing the hat out the window and into the East River. I pictured the hat flowing north into the Long Island Sound, covered in spotted moon snails, befriending a sea grape. Carlo had nothing more to say about his ex-girlfriend. One deep awkwardness filled the room. Even your corrupt kitchen couldn't hold so many of us and when it seemed we'd reached the meaning of capacity the doorbell rang. Barry scampered to it, being the most recent kitchen arrival, the closest still to the door. "Mendelson!" we heard him exclaim.

BUTTER

MENDELSON TURNED OUT TO BE ONE OF THE SPECTACULARLY FIT older gentlemen who could model quarter-zip trail tees for the L.L. Bean Signature Collection. A breed of preternatural athletes sixty-five and older who redirect the savings of a corporate lifetime into elderly oomph. The first signal of Mendelson's health is his haircut: tight on the sides, gray everywhere, and wonderful on top. The second signal is his neck: he likes you to see his neck. Finally, his socks, which are brave and patterned and knit from single-origin wool. This is a man who has touched mastery and who now spends his time restraining himself from tasteless expenditure. This is Carlo's dream and it stood there right in front of him. Carlo stared at Mendelson as you'd stare at an armadillo.

"Good of you to come," said Barry, who looked so proud of his life he could die.

"How's Betty?" Carlo asked. "Still dancing?"

"Don't get him started on Betty!" Barry said, taking Mendelson's coat. "She was welcome to join you tonight, you know." Barry walked off toward the closet and Carlo leaned close to Mendelson and whispered, "Go on, get started."

The fact is these mature men love the shit out of their second wives. Betty positively rescued them. Before Betty, they were misunderstood. Psychically lonely and imperfectly loved. Before Betty, all they had was cash. Now they have cash and Betty.

We all joined you at the table except Mendelson, who asked to use the restroom. We original six sat in petrified silence, waiting to say some kind of grace. You stood, as if you were she. You rushed to the kitchen and came back with cloth napkins, coiled up into bamboo napkin rings. We passed them around. You sat again, and the impossibility of grace resumed. Then, once more, the doorbell.

"There's nobody else," you said vaguely, and Barry again rushed to the door.

Carlo's generally orderly face filled with mischief, his expression deadpan and his eyes entertained. A man in a blue mechanic's jumpsuit stood in the hallway, propping up a giant plastic-wrapped mattress.

Barry looked back to the table in astonishment. Carlo removed his napkin from its ring. The delivery man slapped the mattress and said, "Where?"

"I bought Nell a bed," Carlo said.

You only raised your eyebrows and said, "Drop it on the floor."

The man pulled this icon of intercourse into the foyer. He dropped it. The mattress squashed all the nice lilies still strewn over the floor and popped berry juice all over its plastic and the large noise shook your cabinets. Barry signed his receipt, tipped him in cash, and in shock wished him a merry Christmas.

"Merry Christmas," said the delivery man as he walked hugely unburdened back down the hall.

Tom, who had been communing with the wallpaper, blinked into consciousness. He slapped Carlo's back as hard as the man had slapped my new bed and smiled and said, "She needed one."

"I know," said Carlo. "Overdue."

"Why is it *here*?" was Mishti's excessively practical question.

"It shouldn't be," Carlo said very mildly, "unless I pasted this address by mistake—Joan's invite came in as I was ordering."

"It's fine," you said, as if a guest had merely broken a wine glass. "If you don't mind, Amanda will lie on it." I couldn't believe your cool. For one second you flickered. "Where have you been sleeping?" you asked me.

I looked at you with weight. It felt like walking on your back. Amanda herself, tall and red, walked into the room, climbed aboard the mattress, sniffed its plastic, spun three times, and collapsed. She let out a great dog sigh. We saw the strip of light under the bathroom door flick off. Mendelson, we thought, in unison. He pulled the door in toward himself, stepped out of the bathroom, caught the tip of his Merrells under the mattress side and fell, face first, onto Amanda.

The dog yelped a human sound and scrambled out from under him. She ran into the kitchen and slurped frantically from her water bowl. The bowl screeched against the floor tile.

Carlo and Tom stood up then didn't move.

Barry shouted, "Hoo!"

Mishti looked at me with eyes that said, *We were young and now we're idiots*. I was born old and have always been an idiot. Mishti stood.

You remained seated and raised both hands to your parted lips and held them there in exhausted, abiding nihilism.

Mendelson lay where he'd landed. Nobody helped him up, he was beyond help, to help would be further insult. He lay there and smelled the mattress's buttons as Amanda had done. Then, slowly, he pressed his palms down and with his established upper-body strength did a kind of push-up into a child's pose, then to kneeling, to squat, to standing. The plastic creaked a fart noise under each of his movements. His head, as they instruct you, was the last to come up.

"Excuse me," Mendelson said neatly, his pranayama-trained low blood pressure boiling somewhere very deep under his skin. He took his seat at the table with the incredible lightness of a man who finds humiliation boring.

I said, "What's the preferred disciplinary action against unsafe mattresses these days? Mr. Estlin, Mr. Mendelson, I appeal to you, couldn't we have this mattress expelled?"

You said, "Nell."

Barry said, "That's hardly funny."

It seemed clear that I had ruined everyone's life. I didn't know what to do or say that could explain the fact that I'd never even asked for anything.

"Sorry!" I shouted at my bamboo napkin ring.

Tom said, "Huh?"

"I mean, thank you!" I shouted at Carlo.

You said, "Stop shouting."

Carlo smiled as if he'd won a thumb wrestle and crooned, "You're welcome."

I poured the wine. Carlo swirled his glass, tasted it, didn't like it, and said it was good. Mishti drank hers in a gulp and then sat back in her chair so that the rest of the night might happen to her.

Mendelson recovered entirely and made a toast, thanking Barry for guiding him to the honorary position, thanking Joan for the potatoes. Barry clanked everyone's glass with sloppy hollow noises. I raised a toast to your pollen-pistil grant. You looked embarrassed to exist. I said I couldn't wait to assist your study. I said your grant would not only earn you tenure, it would save my life. Heat rose from radiators before the great bay window and made the glass panes look molten and swirling. The apartment itself swallowed my toast, and the power and congratulation you deserved that night crumbled submissively under the outdated thumb of Riverside Drive. Barry said, "Hear hear." You thanked him, barely moving your lips.

Anyone who has something you want—a talent, a beauty, an apartment—is paying for it at a price you may find intolerable. Joan what I wish for you even more than I wish myself for you is that you find someone who has only what they need. You'll find they haven't paid for it, the world has given it to them in deference to the humility of their request. This is a person who can weather life and who can rejoice in it.

Your sweet potatoes tasted like apple butter.

WINE

AFTER I CLEARED THE TABLE, THE BED WAS STILL ON THE FLOOR, WE
no longer noticed it, it had become something natural to the space.
Amanda occasionally revisited it, as if taking herself on vacation.
Carlo opened a Sancerre he'd brought for the hosts but hadn't pre-
sumed to pair with the meal; he found new glasses in your sturdy
cupboards and poured the bottle out between us. In an adolescence-
flavored stupor we receded into assorted corners and drank there,
raised the low music, checked in to an evening we knew would turn
jolly and damaging. There is no upper age limit for electing damage. It's not a youth folly but a heart folly.

Mendelson was twirling a what, a toothpick? An extra-long
toothpick? Somewhat acrobatically from finger to finger and rubbing Amanda (they now knew each other well) with the side of his
calf. Carlo and Mishti flanked him, nodding.

"December," someone said, as if all night we'd been singing one
song and this was the song's name.

"And the hysterical year-end crunch."

I wandered past to find you and Carlo stopped me and said, "No
one should sleep on the floor." It occurred to me now that Carlo
had spent, you know, some money, that the bed had *cost* something, though its price seemed to hover somewhere above Mishti's
head in an abstract nondollar denomination.

"Thank you, Carlo," I said. "It's—"

"She's been sleeping on the floor," Carlo said to Mendelson.

"I gathered," Mendelson said with that old bored knife-light in his eyes. He shook my hand and said, "Congratulations," as if I'd closed a merger, and I stroked the inside of his palm with my middle finger until he jumped. I looked at Mendelson's exposed neck and said, "Don't worry, there is rest for the wicked," and turned and shook Carlo's hand and said, "Thanks," and Carlo said, "Please." He took Mishti's hand warmly and adoringly. Mishti looked down and stroked Amanda's spine. Mendelson rubbed his palm against the side of his hip to remove the feeling of me. I didn't care that he had disciplined me. He occurred to me now as a dustpan.

"I'm looking forward to Bermuda," she said. She seemed so tired.

"Bermuda?" Mendelson asked. "Why Bermuda? Or I suppose, when?"

"When? Christmas," said Carlo.

"Nice," Mendelson said, the most bored he'd been yet. "I was going to recommend you to the holiday colloquium," you could see Carlo's soul curdle in his eyes, "but the beach is more relaxing."

"Bermuda—" Carlo started, as if he wanted to say that there were no beaches on Bermuda and he couldn't.

"Gorgeous," Mendelson said. "Anyway the colloquium is for joyless maniacs with a single-track mind. I'm glad you have some joy in your life." This seemed more or less earnest, if simultaneously devastating. "Betty would love Bermuda, but . . . she understands."

And I watched Mishti internalize this understanding, catch the punt, and take a knee, knowing it was now her turn to understand, to permit, to forfeit, to encourage Carlo to go ahead and have a single-track mind, darling.

I couldn't bear it and it wasn't my business and I walked into the library, you have a library in your home, and you weren't there. I stood alone in the cavernous, overstuffed den and understood what it is to be a chipmunk.

When I turned back to see how Mishti looked, I saw Barry refill her glass, this time red, from a new bottle he'd conjured and opened. Something bottomless yawned under us, everyone could feel it, an infinite river of wine had thawed and arrived to cut through our winter. Mishti drank the glass so quickly Barry could refill it before he kept walking. Tom appeared, it seemed out from under the floor. Then, soon, you. I couldn't resist the group; it was cold in the den. I walked back toward Mishti and she shrank away toward a console on the far wall. A few quiet seconds followed in which I couldn't see her face or her hands. Then she began to sing.

WATER

THE SONG POURED FROM BARRY'S SOUND SYSTEM AT A VOLUME that could carbonate water. Mishti faced the wall, back to us. She extended her right arm out to the side and twirled it just the way it's twirled in our movie. I knew what was happening even before I could believe it. One very specific part of our life was coming to the front of our life. She had nothing left to give but this central treasure she carried at all times and never gave. Her upright neck, from behind, looked like a soldier's. On the next line she turned to face us, as the woman in pink does, and sang the rest of the verse with the accompanying dance move: hand ripples under the eyes. In the movie, Hrithik Roshan watches her dance and slowly walks toward her. I knew more forcefully than ever who I was. I slowly walked toward her. She walked toward me. We met on the mattress.

Mishti knew who I was too. I stood before her in Hrithik's crossed-arm posture and she rotated her wrists on either side of my face. The mattress wobbled beneath us.

"Le jaa le jaa!" we simultaneously wailed. *"Soniya le jaa le jaa!"*

It meant: Take away, my beloved, take it away!

Mishti sang the pink woman's solo *Oh* with both arms outstretched.

Tom stared at us as if we'd become planets.

We knew the dance. We knew every step of the dance. I had no idea bodies could memorize anything so well. We were terrible and inebriated and the plastic-wrapped mattress was less grounding than the surface of the moon but it was the deluxe moment when your external life sees your internal life and therefore sees you at your best. The Hindi lyrics I'd heard hundreds of times burst from my lips like a formula. The men stared at us, as if we'd seizured. Our accidentally identical outfits looked like a uniform for our ceremony. There was one move that required the ardent wiggling of our thumbs. We wiggled our thumbs in unbelievable sync. We were doing the most elaborate rib cage contractions and shoulder pumps and a touch of fancy footwork I'd never before dared but could do now because Hrithik had done it, with us, for us, so many nights on the couch. Around two minutes into the song an instrumental interlude hit and we collapsed onto the patient mattress. As with Mendelson's fall, nobody applauded, or commented, or moved.

We closed our eyes, lying on our backs, heaving on the mattress, our necks sweating onto the plastic. I wanted you to think of me as delightful. I know you aren't interested in delight. I thought you might be interested in humiliation. I wasn't embarrassed. I was very, very proud. Mishti created and filled the cavity beside me and I felt newly grateful to Carlo for such an excellent bed, a bed I'd be honored to sleep in, now that it'd been so christened. Someone approached us, it was Tom. He offered his hand to Mishti. She took it and stood up. Nobody helped me up, or everyone assumed I wanted to keep lying there. I kept lying there. Carlo and Barry and Mendelson came over to stand with Tom and I looked at these four male heads above me as if they were the north, south, east, and west winds.

"Mendelson's got a great idea," Carlo said, above me, to Mishti. "You take Betty's dance intensive, I'll take the colloquium, and we go to Bermuda in February."

Tom walked away. You followed him. Mishti excused herself to the restroom. Mendelson had to be going. Barry walked him to the elevator. Carlo went somewhere I couldn't see. My new bed has sixteen buttons, four hundred coils, and a pillow top. Amanda came and lay next to me in the spot Mishti had warmed.

MEAT

AMANDA SMELLED LIKE BEEF MIXED WITH TURKEY SERVED OVER polenta. She panted her breath at me and I welcomed it. I have been panting my polenta breath at everybody for thirty-one years and nobody has ever welcomed it. Her red unwashed fur washed itself in little clumps here and there across her belly. I congratulated her on her mammalhood. Neither of us apologized. Amanda drooled the way I like to drool, down one side of the mouth, it dripped onto her left paw and polished her claws, and I knew right then that I could be acceptable, to her, and to myself, if not to you.

SALT

EVERYTHING HAD BECOME POSSIBLE NOW THAT I COULD DANCE AND I owned a bed and I'd parted with my last shred of privacy, the words *balls to the wall* rang through my blood as if chimed from church bells, so when Mishti's face appeared above mine dripping ink onto my forehead I didn't register any *surprise*. Surprise had left our party. I didn't even feel concern. I felt a kind of strawberry-colored curiosity.

Having finally, slowly, Mendelson-style stood up, I faced Mishti and found her crying. Her explicitly un-waterproof mascara had ruled her face into columns. She didn't attempt to wipe anything off her cheeks or nose or heart-shaped chin. I'd never seen her cry and now learned that when she did it, she did it with uncurbed exuberance. I couldn't help but try to wipe something. I ran the back of my hand under her nose and pulled some swirly snot away from her. Now that she could breathe, she opened her mouth and said, "I never believed you."

I didn't blame her, I'd never believed me either, but in a specific sense I didn't know what she was talking about. "That's okay," I said, to be overarching about it.

"But it's actually worse now, believing you is worse."

"Huh," I said. She took my hand and walked me toward your library.

Tom had you pushed up against the glass cabinet doors of your rare books collection: your leg wrapped around his knee and your arm wrapped around his ass. Mishti and I watched you two clean each other's teeth outside of time and space and then I pulled Mishti into the bathroom. I shut the door behind us and couldn't find the light switch. A small, wild-rose-shaped nightlight plugged in above the sink gave off a pink light, a glow that filled the sink and bounced off the porcelain onto the ceiling. At the moment it seemed perverse to me that you'd be afraid of the dark. There had been something unidentifiably dark about the library: it wasn't about Tom, it wasn't about Barry, it wasn't even about you—it had to do with desperation.

Mishti closed the toilet lid, sat down, and proclaimed: "Tom is the most spiritually lazy and emotionally selfish man I've ever met and my entire being resents him and I don't know how to bear the way he simply doesn't want me."

Joan I needed you then in the bathroom, I wasn't of sound mind and this was a little too much for me. Also I could hardly see. Mishti's neck was light level and became the room's one pink pillar. Didn't want her?

"Which is to say—" I stammered.

"I want him," she finished.

"I had no idea," was the whole truth and the only thing I could say.

"It was okay when he was with you because you come first, for me, and you met him first, and sense made sense, it was fine, but then you didn't even like him, and I couldn't stand watching it— how did you stay together so long?"

"I'm not sure," I idly grabbed the faucet handle, "I think he felt like protection to me? And I felt like nothing to him, which was all he was looking for." Tom, now that I thought of it, had to be Mishti's perfect complement: perfect and complement both in the sense of achieving wholeness. He was abstract, imprecise, dreamy, and un-ambitious; she was exact and earthbound; they were both beauti-ful. Tom and I had shared no such symmetries. We had both been underwhelmed, underspoken, dry, and polite. I turned the faucet on and the cold water rushed out. Mishti turned it off.

I asked her why she wanted him. It seemed worth asking. She had prepared, as she would, a comprehensive and sensible answer: she loved how little direction he needed, how self-generative and flexible he was, loved the prettiness of his impractical degree, and his unapologetic dilettantishness, which in her eyes revealed his fluency in all the assorted flavors of the world she'd never in her rigidity know. She loved him because he was relaxed, sophisticated, and odd. She saw who he was and loved him for it.

You don't love Tom like this. What you don't feel for Tom is what Mishti feels in torrents: clear arrows of appreciation for Tom's totally bland interior. It sets her mind at ease. It means nothing to you. I wondered if you would give Mishti your seat, as if she were pregnant, or disabled. I knew you wouldn't, because you ultimately wouldn't want to insult her, because you consider unearned giving a cheap shot. I used to think Mishti wouldn't take the seat, either, but I'd never seen her like this. She sat in black on the toilet, pink and in love with Tom.

I replayed your make-out against the bookshelf. That raging at-traction between you and Tom seemed to run on disbelief, as if each had surprised the other with the gift of a new and not neces-sarily inhabitable continent. Joan I felt so angry. Not because Tom had beaten me to you, not because you had beaten Mishti to Tom, not because you had invited us into your home and then hacked down your ceiling while we were trapped inside, but because you had given up your own elegance and your elegance is all I believed in. You had turned clumsy, and rude. Break my heart as many times as you want, but who are you to break Mishti's? She stood and washed the mascara from her cheeks. I left her there and went in search of Barry.

LEATHER

"WHAT'S YOUR MOVE," I SAID. I'D COME ALL THE WAY DOWN TO THE lobby to find him and had lost my mind in the elevator. He stood chatting with the doorman as if his life weren't changing. The doorman said, "Evening."

"Your *move*," I said. "Who do you fight for? Your wife? Your girlfriend? Yourself?"

"Fight?" said Barry. He wasn't ready to part with the earnestly pleasant time he'd been having and knew me to be unpleasant. He looked at me the way you might look at a telemarketer you could see.

"I'm sorry to interrupt. Tom and Joan are having a go of it in the library and Mishti is having a good cry and you're down here with," I squinted at the doorman's name badge, "Charles. I thought you might want a piece of the action."

"*A go of it?*" said Barry. I wondered how many years on earth you could complete by only repeating the last thing someone else said to you. Barry had completed forty-five.

I walked back through the parallel leather couches and rang the elevator bell. Barry whispered something disparaging to Charles and then jogged over to the elevator door as it was opening. We rode the first nine floors in silence. Between the ninth and tenth floors Barry asked me, "Do you think she knows about Mishti?" I didn't answer. "She must," he said. "Christ, she must have known all along." A blissful, luminous fear poured through me, as if fear were the cousin of justice.

TIME

"JOAN," SAID BARRY.

"Barry," said Tom.

"I'm sorry," Barry said, taking a left turn. "Joan from my heart I'm so sorry."

"You're sorry?" said Mishti, clean-faced.

"I'm sorry," Barry said to Mishti as well.

"I'm not," you said to everyone.

Tom said nothing.

"Babe," said Carlo. Nobody knew where he'd come from.

"I don't want to go to Bermuda," said Mishti.

"February," said Carlo.

"Not ever," said Mishti.

"Do you mean—" said Carlo.

"I mean," said Mishti.

"It'll never happen again," said Barry.

"You can have whatever you like," you told him.

"I want you," said Barry.

"I want him," you said.

Tom said nothing.

I looked at you and the difference between age forty and thirty and fifteen felt very small. We all stood awaiting the day we'd grow up and leave home.

LOVE

IN YOUR OFFICE A WEEK LATER YOUR BRAID WAS BACK. YOU LOOKED at me and said, "Why did you fetch Barry, you idiot dog."

"Why did you flaunt Tom?"

"When beauty asks you a question, how often do you reply?"

"Joan," I said, "Joan," I had conquered you forever and now you'd have to die of shame, "Joan," I said, moaning the *o*, "are you quoting Ani DiFranco at me?"

You took a seat, humbly, in complete defeat.

"Yeah," you said. I'd never heard you say *Yeah* before. You smiled. You said, "I thought she was before your time."

"We're the same," I said, and added, for good measure, "I need you."

"How do you need me, Nell."

"As a parent."

"I chose not to have children."

"As a teacher."

"Expelled."

"As a friend."

"You have several."

"As an institution."

"Enroll anywhere else."

"As validation."

"I have validated you."

"As approval."

"I don't approve."

"As the only person beside myself I can bear."

"You can bear yourself?"

"Now I can't."

"Good, go home."

I started to cry, which I hadn't done since Tom's string beans and before that not for four years.

You grimaced at my feelings and said, "I'm tired of you and all your little friends pawing at me as if I can bless you, I can't bless you, leave me the motherfuck alone."

"Leave Barry," I said.

"I did," you said.

I grabbed the armrests of your chair and kissed you. The chair squeaked. I held the roller wheel in place with one foot. You leaned back and rested your head on the wall.

"I don't love you," you said.

I let go of the armrests and the wheel. I must have looked frazzled. You said, to be clearer, "I am not in love with you, Nell Barber," and it was the kindest and most legitimizing thing you could say, as if you could have loved me, as if you only happened not to, as if you only didn't, not couldn't, not wouldn't dare.

"We've come to the end of this now," you said, your eyelids hanging so low on your coldest eyes you might have been half asleep. "I'll send you the assistant money and registration when it comes through this week. Test your monkshood. Leave me out of it. You're fine, Nell. I'm fine. We're the same. As you've said: get a goddamn grip."

MEMO

From:
NSF Aid Committee
Office of the Chairman

To:
Professor Joan Kallas
Columbia University

Your applicant for the assistant position has been rejected, as it has been brought to our attention that she is ineligible. Assistants must be currently enrolled doctoral candidates working toward a terminal degree in your project's most closely aligned field. Please resubmit an enrolled and qualified candidate by January 15 for reconsideration. Thank you.

Nell—
I should have expected this, I didn't think
they had the most updated registrar logs.
I'm sorry. There's nothing else I can do for
you and I'd rather we stop speaking.
You understand.

My best, J

MARCH

I empty myself of my life and my life remains.

MARK STRAND

I

LOSE ME AS YOU LOST YOUR CAT, YOUR BEARINGS, YOUR WHERE-
withal, your identity. Lose me as you lose autumn each year to ice,
as you lose a year each year. Lose me as you lose a little weight and
your bones show. Lose me like a wet food dropped face down. Both
earrings. Any key. Lose me like what blew off the ferry. Lose me like
the dollhouse furniture you kept since childhood and in adulthood
misplaced while moving. Lose me like your prize mountain you
saw once and can't remember where it was, what country. Lose me
the way you lose fog. Lose me and fuck you.

I am the field that cannot comprehend itself after the fog has
cleared and it is only itself again. I am the fog that has cleared. I
am the cleanest, smallest, emptiest land mammal and I am fast.
I am not waiting for anyone to come. Take your years, your rituals,
your favorites and your signs, I have none of you. I give you entirely
back to yourself and I know that is more than you want.

It is completely sacred to lose something you never needed.

The anger that takes your place is red and unnecessary but
I'll lose it too in turn and then only my nonphysical self will fill up
my physical self, I'll be exactly my whole size. I will not be 40 percent you.

It's March again, last year on this date you analyzed my oaks,
time circles but it does not repeat, March again but no oaks. It is up
to me to do something today that I might like to recall on this date
next year. You are no longer my marker of time.

I regret your bloodlessness, your peace, your instruction, your friendship, your hair, your socks I never saw.

I want to be your nothing, to occur to you only as an unknown, for your only thought of me to be wonder, not wonder as awe but as an absolute lack of information.

Not to impress, not to receive your approval your interest or your disdain, total blankness, which is not to say that we are strangers, it is to say that we have fallen from each other's grace.

Some things are just very large parts of your life, and not your life.

If you change your life it changes. I changed my life and it changed. My life did not assert itself (or it did, as pain) or hold fast or keep shape.

I have only ever been a crayon.

The hymn says: I am like one who has been anointed.

The train says: Stand clear of the closing doors.

HILDEGARD

HILDEGARD VON BINGEN, YOU PROPHET, YOU DOCTOR, YOU ABBESS, you hearer of music, you daughter of the Nahe River, you daughter of Hildebert, you ward of Jutta the sister of Count Meginhard, you wearer of the habit of a nun, you favorite of the monk Godfrey and the abbot Conon, you articulator of the cosmos that holds humanity between thumb and forefinger, you composer of canticles, you creator of nine hundred words, you baker of spelt bread, you will be my new Joan.

I dedicate this third notebook to you and I take your teachings as its start. I couldn't keep up with things the way they were. I couldn't keep up with Joan. I couldn't keep up with my so-called self. I couldn't even maintain my own system. I saw Joan's tongue in Tom's mouth and forgot the foods, my favorite, and collapsed without thinking into cop-outs like Leather, Time, Love? As if Love had anything to do with what happened in the arms of Joan's swivel chair. No more monikers, euphemisms. In this book we go back to ourselves. I am Nell. You are Hildegard.

You say,

Peas make a person courageous.
Eating watercress is not of much use or much harm to a
person.
When eaten, parsnip only fills the person's stomach.

I say, give me peas.
You say,

In whatever way it is eaten, fennel makes a person happy.
In whatever way it is eaten, dill makes a person sad.
In whatever way it is eaten, celery induces a wandering mind since its greenness sometimes harms and makes the person sad with instability.

I say, I have eaten enough celery for four lifetimes and let the fifth be flavored by fennel. I say, enough dill.
You say,

Chick-peas are warm and gentle.
Bitter vetch is not very suitable as a medicine.

I say, indeed.
You say,

If a person goes out of his or her mind as if they know nothing and are lying deranged in ecstasy, dip peony seed in honey and place it upon the tongue.

You said this between 1152 and 1158, almost a millennium before I went out of my mind. I always know nothing. You never saw me lying deranged in ecstasy (I have lain deranged in ecstasy). Still you knew me, because you knew every being who had been or would be. You argued in 1152 for whole grains, for ginger as a digestion aide, for butter and salt in moderation. I didn't know, as far into the future as yesterday, that nutmeg will calm all the bitterness of heart and mind, open the clouded senses, and make the mind joyful. I didn't know that hail never falls on a fern. You say to put a rose leaf on my eye in the morning. Hildegard, I will.

You say,

Let a person in whom melancholy rages, who has a bitter soul, and who is always sad, often drink wine cooked with arum root; the melancholy and fever will diminish.

I say, we can do this together, this new year. Neither you nor Elvis died. But I don't know where to get any arum root.

You say,

Let whoever's head is crusty cut off the soft part of bacon and also its rind and throw away these parts. Then let the person take the rest, pound it with calendula in a mortar, and smear the head with it often. The crustiness will fall off, and the person's head will be beautiful.

I say, give me bacon. I say, my head will be beautiful.

SUNNY

FOR THE PAST TWO MONTHS IN THE ABSENCE OF ANY OTHER STRUC-
ture or form of support I have worked the bar at Sunny's. I work
twelve-hour shifts because the bar is only open twelve hours a day.
Johansen can't understand my devotion but she's no longer under-
staffed so she finally got to fire George. She's always wanted to fire
George. I wish George were still around. He was conscientious
about filling the peanut bowls. Every Monday I buy three groceries:
yogurt, rigatoni, and Birds Eye frozen vegetables. There are times
in your life when tortellini becomes painful. I do yogurt for breakfast, yogurt for lunch, and rigatoni and vegetables for dinner
wherein the vegetables are souped up in yogurt. I don't cook meat
at home because it's expensive and it never washes off. Every once
in a while I fry bacon to communicate with Hildegard. In any case
I'm getting enough protein.

Whoever coined the term "make a living" poetically misled us.
It's bad math to equate life with survival. I am making a living behind the bar. I am not living, or feeling alive. I've started water-
flossing again.

In this same two-month period Carlo has started a hedge fund.
The seed money came from a friend of Mendelson's friend. Barry
has left the university; he has joined Carlo; his new title is COO,
which is a sound I like to make out loud and think of him making.
Joan has left everybody. No one has heard from Joan.

That colloquium Carlo attended while Mishti did not attend

Betty's Shake-Off-Christmas dance intensive has an odd name considering it has nothing to do with academic seminars and everything to do with pairing investment managers with launch capital. Carlo went to Bermuda by himself in February and came up with the fund name there: Juniperus, after the Latin name for the Bermuda cedar tree. Sometimes I wonder if Carlo, provider of beds and namer of trees, shared more of my interests than I realized. I doubt I'll see him again. It's nice that he wanted an earth-inspired name for his hedge fund but Juniperus sounds more like a planetary mix of Jupiter and Uranus and I find it hard to pronounce. I hope his investors find it winning. I don't actually wish Carlo any harm. It's most likely that Carlo, in eventually losing his investors' money, will be the source of his own damage, which makes sense, because nothing else has ever damaged Carlo.

I'm sorry that the one thing he wants is something he's not going to get. The one thing he wants is to be dazzlingly rich, and he is only smart enough to be tolerably rich. Dazzling riches require some real imagination. I wish for him that he might someday come to want another thing. That's the real hazard with people who only wish for one thing in the world: the brutal singularity of the wish doesn't make them any more likely to get it. And when they don't get it, they are no longer people. Carlo's going to be blank for a long time before he waltzes again and I do hope he waltzes again.

Barry is taking care of Carlo's "operations," which again sounds more like bowel movements to me than whatever it's supposed to suggest. He's very sad to have lost his marriage but I don't think he's more sad than he's happy to have gotten this job. He's escaped academia for all time; he'll be consequential now, and welcome among the consequential. His new crowd will be full of his next wives.

Mendelson promises him as much. But more immediately, I'm sure Barry has a few recent graduates in mind. They too have just left the university. They too need a hand to hold.

Mishti no longer holds Barry's hand, or Carlo's, or anyone's. She won't allow any more sex. Mishti used to believe, believe fervently, that hard work will be rewarded, and beauty will be desired, and that being wonderful is worth it. Since the smut of our Christmas dinner, she's taken up new theories: liars win, lust is disgusting, trust is impossible. This kind of total ideological crash is only available to those who are capable of fervent belief in the first place. Mishti used to hold colossal faith in the great glow of the world; she's now colossally depressed. Her gates have crashed down around her, like before a battle: her eyes are closed, fists are closed, lust is closed, ears are closed even to sympathy. She's turned herself off, as if with the flipping of a power switch, and really, I cannot see her lights anymore. She is miring in a kind of hate—who knows how long this stupor will last—hate of passion, hate of connection. She finds love ludicrous. She says that love is only vanity, delusion, and greed. She says she doesn't want any part of it. I have heard her say she wants to die.

Mishti is too alive to die, but she's making a pretty good show of it. She's started skipping class, as if rebellion were only now occurring to her, at age twenty-six. She's removing the enormous jewels from her fingers and lifting her bare middle finger to the world.

I'd like to return to the world, if it will have me. In Joan's words, I'd like to get something done. My one sprouting castor bean is rising a little higher every day; the other is still dormant. I'd like to test and treat the soil of my monkshood potting, adjust the pH, give it the supplemental nutrients it may need to get going. All I need is one good leaf and then I can literally turn it. Maybe when I finish Rachel's project, this project that was never even mine, I can decide what my own project will be. It won't be oaks, maybe it won't even be a biological science. Maybe Mishti and I will give it all up and start from scratch. Start a taco truck. A scarf store. A pillow factory. Joan would finally implode in disappointment. Good, I would like that.

Hildegard, have you heard from Joan?

BARBER

MY PARENTS CALLED ME. I GUESSED THAT SOMEONE NECESSARILY had died, but they only wanted to say hello. Hello is not something we say in our family.

"Hello," I said.

"It's a new year," my father said. Even pre-coffee math insisted that it had been a new year for at least seventy-five days.

I put the coffee on and thought, My father is only one-half Jewish. His mother, one Esther Rosenbaum of Albany, NY, married to her mother's infinite discontent Harry Barber, the hat man. ("Hat man?" I once asked. "He sold some kind of hats" is all I've ever been told.) But Esther, in allegiance to her mother or to protect herself from vanishing, became Jewisher and Jewisher with time, bar mitzvah–ing my father so thoroughly he can still recite the haftorah blessing by heart. The hat man didn't mind.

"It's March," I said.

"My flowers will be out soon," said my mother, who must have been holding the extra handheld in the kitchen.

The truth is I'd forgotten about my mother's garden. One way I have never thought of her is as a gardener. I have thought of her as a geophysicist, which is what both she and my father were until their retirement. Having borne so little in-person witness to their retirement as I have, I guess I missed her point. Her point about new interests, which happened to be my interests, translated, humanely, from my sour theoretics into her totally wholesome daylight.

"What kind of flowers you got, Ma," I said. This was already the longest conversation we'd had in I don't know how long and it astonished me.

"Well," I could see the little frown between her eyebrows, "daffodils, but I know that isn't interesting."

Heaven bless Kansas, I thought, what is interesting?

"They're going to come up nicely," said my father. "Nicely nicely Johnson."

"I'm planting monkshood," something at the depth of my knees rose up and said completely without my permission.

"You're kidding," my mother said, and I thought she was definitely right. "Ellen told me not yesterday that she wanted to plant a patch of monkshood for the color of them, you know, just a little blue here and there," I looked up from the floor out the window into dilated purple Red Hook and thought *Just a little blue here and there*, "but she's frightened of them, you know, because they say they've got such poison."

"They do," I said, gently, which felt to me like saying *Happy Birthday Ma, You're a Very Nice Lady*. "But she can plant them for the color no problem," I said, "no problem, tell her only not to eat any."

"Eat any!" said my mother.

"She can call you," my father said, "can't she Nell? Ellen Bailey? I've already gone and told her you're the expert in such things."

I must be getting very, very old now. I took a long drink of coffee. It had come to this: my father's recommending my services to his neighbor was without question the most gratifying thing that had ever happened to me in my life.

"You bet," I said. I wondered if in my father's mind's eye I still had turquoise rubber bands on my braced buck teeth, or my signature jumbo forehead and girl-mullet and man-socks, and whether he had ever considered me beautiful. I wondered if he had ever seen me kissing a photograph of Kevin Bacon in the back of our barn, and I found myself hoping he had. I wondered if he had ever wished unattainable things for me, like prosperity and a sweetheart. All at once I couldn't remember a single conversation we'd ever had. I could remember my mother's red winter gloves.

"Always thought you were good at talking to folks," said my father. "Always thought you'd grow up a talking doctor, you know, a psychiatrist? Psychologist."

"What's with everyone and the psychologists?" I said. I could still see Chardonnay's mauve lipstick mouthing *Melt your head.*

"Well they're reckoned to be good for your health," said my father.

"I'll talk to Ellen Bailey," I said.

"That's fine," said my mother.

"Nicely nicely Johnson," said my father, his expression of choice. I laughed and spilled coffee all over my arms. I could remember Frank Sinatra and Marlon Brando and a woman whose name I never felt the need to know, on the cover of a VHS tape of *Guys and Dolls*, on top of their TV credenza.

"Oh and Nell, your cousin Richard is going in for his surgery, they can't put it off any longer," my mother said as I was trying to lick the coffee off my elbow. "Would you write to him? A card, a postcard," she said. There, I thought, and despised myself, a regular

elbow licker, for making Richard sick, for making him sick by assuming that somebody had to be sick. It could have just been her
garden she was calling about. It couldn't have just been her garden.

"Oh sure," I said. "A card."

"He's all right," said my father. It wasn't true, for as much as he
meant it.

"That's fine," my mother said.

After the call I went out and bought a rug. A small rug to put on
the floor under the windows. I sat down there a long time and
thought—we come from somewhere, we really do.

KALLAS

I TOLD JOAN'S FATHER NO COFFEE, NONE FOR ME, I'D ALREADY HAD coffee at home thanks. He didn't remember who I was and asked if I'd rather have tea.

"All right," I said.

"Gray?"

"Lemon?"

"You got it." He was an old man who put his entire enthusiasm into expressions like *You got it*, into events like a lemon tea. I could tell I was going to have a great time with him and that I would probably cry. When he came back with my cup I wanted to keep him at my end of the counter—five stools down an elderly woman ate scrambled eggs and didn't require any immediate attention.

I said, "What's the diner business like these days?" and he said, "Same as ever. Tenderness, succor, and humility." My tea was still two hundred degrees hot and I sipped at it, razzle-dazzled. "Succor?" I couldn't help repeating. "That's what they call us," he said.

"I'm a friend of your daughter's," I had to say then, because deception was neither tender nor humble. Succor's definition hung about five inches outside my brain.

At that, Konstantinos Kallas opened the cheesecake vault and lifted me a slice of raspberry-topped, crumb-bottomed cheesecake so tall it could change a lightbulb.

"You weren't so familiar for nothing." He handed me a fork and a knife, because I'd be needing real tools.

"I have a very forgettable face."

"Now how's Joan." He closed the vault and leaned on it. "She's going through, wouldn't you say, a hard time, a hard time," he said.

"Hard, probably also right."

"Well he loved her, Barry," I couldn't deny this, I ate my raspberry topping, "even if he was some kind of hot-air balloon."

Joan you got your father's bull's-eye aim for what something is, what it's made of, what it's worth. But he is naturally gladder.

"It's the school mistreated her," he said, "they won't say *come* and they won't say *go*."

"Only traffic guards say those things with any regularity."

"I say *go* all the time," said Konstantinos. Then he said it to a plate of browned home fries ready to leave the heat lamps. A waiter came and got them, took them away. "They owe her a word, one word," he said. I said, "I agree."

"Fact is she stopped trying when Rhea died. Her mother's opinion mattered. Her father's opinion is sour cream." He shrugged his eyebrows in cozy, tired self-loathing.

"You have no idea whether she stopped trying," I said too aggressively, his cheeks flinched into an uncomfortable half-smile, and I adjusted to, "Who could know?"

"I know, I know she cooled it down. Doing well didn't mean so much anymore."

I looked down at the extraordinary volume of cheesecake I'd managed to eat without even tasting it and realized I'd cooled it down. I've stopped trying. It's like I've given up having anything other than a body. I wanted then to go out and run down the length of the stained East River, systematically fatiguing every muscle except the heart.

"What was Rhea like?"

"Smart."

"Smart and?"

"Disappointed."

Somewhere underground in Lawrence, Kansas, Jessica Barber's daffodils prepared for their own birth. I had never disappointed her. I'd also never tried to do her proud. It's because I've never tried that I'm bloodless. It's because Rhea died that you're pale.

"Rhea said academia's for narcissists," he wiped down the counter where a cherry had fallen, "and Barry's a spoiled shit. She wanted Joan to do something sincere, like cure Parkinson's, and have a child." I looked around the diner and its eaters—solitary, cooperative, dingy—a microcosm of a city driven less by capitalism than by our collective need for approval.

"Tell her I'm here anyway," Konstantinos said, "she doesn't speak to me so much anymore."

Joan maybe we haven't been dealing with love here maybe it's been validation. Neither of us has ever felt approved of and so we approved of each other. That's not whole, that's not anything.

I handed him a twenty and he handed it back to me. More eyebrows.

"I just talked to my folks for the first time in several months," I said, and concluded, needlessly, with, "We're all assholes."

He didn't like the vulgarity so much and went to clear the lady's half-eaten eggs. I left then because I hadn't yet told him my name and he'd have no way to tattle on me. I wasn't trying to get in touch with you. I was trying to touch the knob on a closed door. I'll leave him alone now too. It wasn't a great idea.

Joan your mother's name means ease, or flow.

She wasn't disappointed. Who could know?

SINGH

"SHE CAN HARDLY STAND UP," ANJALI POINTED AT MISHTI'S STOMACH with a spatula, "I've never seen her like this."

"Mom," said Mishti.

"She hates sitting still, she used to bite this sofa with her baby teeth."

"Oh?"

"Now she's a human shih tzu," Anjali said, and I pictured that mini-beast: Mishti's face with dense fur between the eyes.

"Let me be," Mishti said. "Let me be a shih tzu."

Anjali looked at me and said, "Do something."

In this post-Joan era nobody says that to me anymore so I found it kind of welcome. I sat in the bay Mishti's fetal posture created, the empty spot where her middle curled away, and fed her a sprig of parsley.

I said, "Where does it hurt?"

She said, "Full-body embarrassed, exhausted, and sick of doing my best." This burnout was overdue.

"Do your worst for a while," I said.

She looked at me with panicked, genuine helplessness and said, "I can't do anything," which for Mishti was the equivalent of "I don't exist." She lifted her head off my leg a little and said, "I give up, I really do, Nell, I give it up, the work, the striving, the unrequited love, the gold stars, the failure, the bullshit, the hurt feelings, the only thing I feel is sick, I feel lazy in a . . . total way. Like to exert myself *in any way* would be to insult the very clear message I am getting from the world or whoever it is shouting: goodbye. Really, Nell, enough, it's a great word: goodbye. Goodbye to this way of being. I've been trying, I've been trying way too hard, I've been fucking any guy I could get, to punish myself for wanting somebody I couldn't have," she said, "and now my body feels punished. Just let me disintegrate. I'll do it quietly, you won't even hear."

Mishti closed her eyes. I wanted to tell her that she could have had Tom, even while he was ostensibly *mine*, because hearts are always up for grabs. But grabbing puts a dent in your dignity, and dignity is Mishti's bag.

She rolled onto her side, her ear up toward my face, and I bent down to it and said, "Don't you *goodbye* me." She had sung me the overachiever's aria and I didn't know how to make her un-sing it. It had been histrionic but so was Mishti, and within the register of Mishti's drama this outburst seemed to come from somewhere eerily deep in her. I felt her shoulder trembling against my thigh, as if she were crying, or freezing. If meeting requirements had always kept Mishti on course, and if she no longer felt compelled to meet them, I no longer knew what would check her energy, what would keep her, in all her cosmic flair, on our modest earthly radar. She covered her head with a pillow. Overachievers who stopped achieving were just . . . over? I looked up.

"I was hoping to ask you a chemical question," I told Anjali but she was walking away. Mishti coiled tighter such that her knees pressed the side of my knees. She didn't say, "Ask *me*," which her non-dog-self would have said. I rested my hands on her knees and told her what I was thinking, which was, "The blessing over the haftorah is nice and melodious."

Mishti didn't pretend to need to respond. I looked up over the back of the sofa and through the transparent curtains which nobody had yet lifted. The G train ride from Carroll Gardens to Queens had been bumpy, as if it wanted to burp me. Under the updated LED subway lighting you can admire people in their least flattering state, which reveals where they're incontestably mighty. I removed the pillow from over Mishti's face and searched for her mightiness.

The stove gas hissed from the kitchen. Anjali hummed a distressed, exultant tune. Between notes she slapped the spatula against her palm. The house smelled like oil. Winter could be wintered this way, with spatulas, with knees, with smoke.

My deflated friend opened her eyes and finally wanted to talk about Tom. I hadn't heard from him since Christmas, and could still picture the pull of his lips as he lifted his face from Joan's and pronounced the single word "Barry." I had nothing to tell her about where he'd gone, or where Joan had taken him. I suggested she seek him out herself. She told me that she'd never seen Tom hold anything as dear as he'd held Joan in the library that night, and she didn't have the strength for a chase.

Without strength, Mishti's love for Tom still carried within it a stubborn conviction that she was *right*, the way she might have been right about sodium's neutron count. Right to love him, right that she loved him, right about her choice and her choice to stick to it. She loved Tom, and to love Tom was the right thing for her to do. I admired Mishti's certainty about this love much more than I admired my own love of certainty.

To distract her from her longing I told her I'd kissed Joan. She asked when, where, I told her, she wasn't for one second surprised and bore into me about the questions I now sat begging.

I don't know, I've never done it before. It felt fine.

I want her the way I want anything I want. Wanted. She's as gone as Tom.

Because of her grace that ignites rivers.

Because of her power that births herds of deer.

"Okay," Mishti said. "You know that if she had left Barry and went off with you she'd be your whole life and you'd be her midlife crisis."

This one hurt and I had nothing to say about it. Mishti looked at me without any fur between her eyes, as if she were completely complete. As if loving Tom were making her ill and entire. As if everything we want that isn't love is a substitute for love, and once the original is there the substitutes feel hopelessly redundant. It was incredible to watch somebody who'd always craved success now suddenly and only crave romance.

"Which is fuller," I whispered to Mishti, "the longing or the union?"

"How could I know?" she said. "I've never felt a union."

"What if being with Tom was more boring than loving him?"

"What if you didn't actually like going down on Joan?"

"What if you found kissing Tom as boring as I did?"

"What if Joan found kissing you as boring as Tom did?"

"What if you're wrong about what you think you want?"

"What if you're wrong about who you think you want?"

Anjali came out of the kitchen.

"How quickly can you bind a toxin to its own antidote," I said without preface, because I didn't want to miss my chance. "I have two giant castor beans planted in my apartment. Could I, chemically speaking, detoxify the ricin in the beans quickly enough to make the detoxification a legitimate remedy?"

"You'd need to leave time for a reaction," Anjali said unambiguously, her daughter's mother.

"Not just a pairing."

"A molecule can't attack itself, it would need to interact and then neutralize."

"Detoxification as an action rather than a state."

Mishti couldn't tolerate this change in subject, she gripped my hand and said, "Would you love me if I were wrecked?" and then walked very weakly toward the bathroom.

"Do whatever you need to do in there," Anjali told her. To me, she said, "Activated charcoal can bind the ricin once it's been digested."

"So you wouldn't die?" Mishti asked, opening the bathroom door.

"No, my baby," said Anjali.

I liked having a mother right there to know better. I liked the way Anjali stood in her own rectangle of window light absolutely unclouded and vivacious, holding an alphonso mango and answering us.

When Mishti closed the door behind her, Anjali sat on the couch as if she'd been standing for twenty-six years and said, "Love can be fought for but not insisted upon."

Joan you bask of crocodiles you cloud of flies you skulk of foxes you smack of jellyfish you tiding of magpies you stud of mares you watch of nightingales you muster of peacocks you nye of pheasants you drift of quail you unkindness of ravens you knot of toads.

Mishti came out of the bathroom twenty minutes later, sobbing. She said you can cry over spilled milk when you *are* the spilled milk. I held her until she ran out of snot, tears, and breath. Anjali and I put her to bed. As I stood in the doorway, boots tied, coat zipped, Anjali rotated her two palms on either side of my ears and then brought them back to herself. It meant something benevolent in her language and I left with my temples buzzing. On the street I could no longer hear Mishti's phlegmy coughing and the absence of it felt disastrous. A handful of rational citizens waited for the G train. Eventually it came, the doors opened, and I was not wrong to want you, Joan, my exaltation of larks.

RACHEL

COULD I HAVE SEEN THE DISASTER, SMALL AS IT MUST HAVE BEEN? Could I have seen the mistake itself? Could I have seen the little annihilation death performed so invisibly, so lightly, we mistook it for air? We called it Thursday afternoon? We gave it no name and went home?

What would I have said?

Don't?

Please? Could I have begged her back from whatever she'd already done? Could I have healed her, heard her, borne her any witness, shoved her beside herself, thrown her the rope of my arm, knocked her off her only path, helped her down from the irreversible? Kissed cure into her mouth? How quickly did it turn too late? How high did the room temperature need to rise to trigger the conditioning that made her sneeze?

I saw her. I saw her and I told myself to "chill the shit out." She wiped her nose on the back of her wrist, her glove rode up, her wrist remained exposed, and I thought, *As if.* As if an Achilles heel is literally a heel, a wrist, a joint. As if we are at the perpetual risk our parents described. As if children should be leashed, dogs should be muzzled, and our snot will lift the hand that lifts the glove that exposes the skin to the toxin that will kill us quickly. As if anything fatal could be dull. As if she were some kind of incompetent. As if I knew better than she did, Rachel Simons, who was older and always so deliberate. The air conditioning had just woken up from

Eco mode. I heard her sneeze and I saw her wipe her nose, so as not to lose a moment of her work, so as to lose the sum total of her moments.

Would I have contained the power, the chemical, the antidote, the understanding, the reflexes, the speed, the dexterity, the brawn, the blessing, to undo her catastrophe? The ability?

I wouldn't have. I could have.

Joan I don't want to be myself anymore I want to be careful.

I want to be perilously honest about loving you.

Rachel Simons was buried in the Green-Wood Cemetery, in Brooklyn, in a plot her parents had purchased the day she was born, because she'd been born unwell and with short expectancy, and they'd wanted to batch the disaster into one big buy. Then Rachel defied all expectations and lived.

After her burial, at the reception, standing beside a hillock of cubed pepper-jack, Tom and I broke up. We didn't deserve life as we knew it, as we lived it, in good health and half heart.

We rode the R train back uptown and transferred at Union Square.

Joan we have grown too chill, we species without fur, we have become shit, we have chilled the shit out, we don't even grow fur over our skin.

PHARMAKON

IN ANCIENT GREEK *PHARMAKON* MEANT POISON *AND* CURE *AND*
scapegoat. It also meant potion and spell and charm. It could mean
artificial color or dye, even paint. It came from roots that meant cut
and throat. The *pharmakon* doesn't change its name whether it's
noxious or healing, whether it destroys or repairs. We assign human value to those results. Go ahead and employ a drug either in
measure, toward health, or in excess, toward oblivion. The *pharmakon* has no intentions; it cooperates.

Pharmakos meant a person sacrificed to atone for a city. If the
sacrifice wasn't killed outright, she was exiled. Once she left town,
the town considered itself pure again.

Theuth, Egyptian god of writing, called writing a *pharmakon*
and he meant a remedy. Writing will help us remember.

Plato called writing a *pharmakon* and he meant a poison. Writing will replace our memories and ruin our minds.

Derrida called writing a *pharmakon* and he meant an ambivalence. Writing is a tool that must be used. How it is used is not
writing's fault, or business.

I am writing this to you in exile, in abject ambivalence, you are
pure again without me, and this writing's effect on your body, if you
ever read this, will be beneficent or maleficent. Ideally both. Your
reaction will be your little godliness, your power to steer me toward
recovery or the end.

BARRY

TODAY BARRY TOOK A SEAT AT MY BAR AND ORDERED HIMSELF A milk stout.

I said, "First time in Brooklyn?"

He said, "I've seen Grand Army Plaza."

I poured his stout and set it down on an Anchor Steam coaster, made in San Francisco since 1896. He rotated the coaster under it, an inch right, an inch left, and wouldn't take a sip.

"How can I help you, Mr. Estlin."

"Mishti said this was a nice bar, it's a nice bar."

"It's a nice bar."

The four thirty sunset came in through three small windows in the door, stretched inward over the bar stools, and landed on his thighs. The counter surface of the bar had become too sunlike to look at plain-eyed. The walls sighed orange. Sunny's, as an institution, had drunk its own air and felt ready for bed. Barry rotated the coaster twice, again.

"I'm not here for any reason, Nell," he said, reasonably, I thought, "or," I waited, "well I can't speak to Joan anymore. So, closest thing is, I thought I'd speak to you." I took his complement and put it right in the bank but Barry and I have no business chumming.

"Where is Joan," I'd go for his information, why not, "have they eloped?"

"Who?"

"What?"

"Tom."

"Oh Tom bailed," he said, as if reporting the weather. "Please. Tom didn't want my forty-one-year-old ex-wife on his hands, when it came down to it. No, no. Come on, Nell. Please."

Please. I played back Tom's lips, his forearms curled between Joan's back and the bookshelf. The way she'd said, "I want him." The way he'd said not a word. I felt Barry had dropped me out of a jet, through a roof, and onto the floor of my pelvis. Clarity consumed me.

"I want your forty-one-year-old ex-wife in my arms," I said.

"You've had her there."

"No, only on my mouth."

I couldn't believe I'd believed Tom to be capable of desire.

Barry said, "She liked Tom's mouth best."

"Tom doesn't have a mouth."

"If a mouthless man goes down on a woman—"

"The woman evaporates."

Joan when you told Barry about my kiss, did you call it torture?

"And she *still* doesn't want anything to do with me," Barry weakly pounded the bar, "that's the real injury. It's just *me*, she just doesn't want *me*, Tom or not. And she sure as hell doesn't want *you*."

I looked out the door windows that grew increasingly magenta.

"She's totally alone," Barry said, "suffering, and she won't even accept my kindness," he said, "she doesn't want a clean start, she wants total painful destruction."

I lifted my phone in a spasm of melodrama and sent Tom the text message: What have you done?

Tom had set out to *get you*, Joan, and was so absolutely pleased that he did. I say this with some meanness in that I'm suggesting he wanted to *get you* more than he wanted *you*, but I'm sure he wanted you too. Maybe once he got you, he wanted you more than he could bear. Maybe once the scaffolding of your unavailability came down, he saw you up close and died. You know, the way Aaron is supposed to keep some distance from the altar of the Lord. I'm not saying you're the Lord Joan don't worry I'm just saying you merit distance.

I know this notebook isn't even about you. I'm sorry, Hildegard. Hildegard, this notebook is still yours. I won't mess it up again.

Barry finally reached for his beer and drank a third of a pint in one sip. He said, "What should I do?"

For the first time I felt attracted to the outright disaster of my castor beans. For the first time I didn't want to neutralize them, didn't want to detoxify them, didn't want to curb their danger, I wanted to deploy them as pure weapon, I wanted their harm, I wanted to harm the man who sat at the bar in front of me. I felt a jolt of disgust run up my neck and squirmed.

"We're filthy," I said. "We're irretrievable."

"Oh, it's smaller than that," Barry said, "I've only ruined my own life."

I paled then because life-ruining is my bag and nobody else's. Joan, I need a new bag. Nobody's life is my business, not even my own. Let the Fates spin their threads. I tried to stop thinking about Barry convulsing and took my hands out of my pockets and returned them to the dusty, harmless air and asked him, "How's business?"

"I don't know anything about business," he said. "But I'll fix the copier as many times as they need." He laughed. "I bet you didn't think I know how to fix a Xerox machine. I do. I'm the only person of any value in that office. The women we've hired are porpoises but someday we'll hire a cutie."

"Remove your love life from my life."

"Oh, go to hell. I thought you'd understand. Don't you hunt pussy these days?"

He finished his beer, paid, and tucked his stool under the bar. "Anyway, business is swell," he said, leaving. He swung an imaginary bat over his shoulder, lowered an imaginary cap over one eye, shrugged, and said, "There's no loving in business."

An old man at the back of the bar whose attendance I hadn't taken hollered mirthfully, "Tom Hanks!"

"Tell Mishti I miss her," Barry said at the door, one side of his face magenta. "She's a hell of a fuck, you should try her."

"I could kill you," I said.

Barry laughed and said, "Back when you had a lab. If Joan's grant was going to save your life, what happens to your life now?"

"That really isn't your business."

"Sure it is. Who do you think told them you aren't enrolled?"

I flung his coaster at him and missed. The nontoxic material world felt hopelessly blunt and soft around its edges. I went home to dig up my castor beans.

TOM

WHILE I WAS WALKING HOME TOM CALLED ME TO APOLOGIZE; I TOLD him to try souping vegetables up in yogurt. He kept saying "I mean it" and I kept saying "crinkled carrots." He kept saying "I'm not even sure where to start" and I kept saying "just put them right in the pot with whichever drained noodle you prefer." After a long time he said he would try the yogurt. I asked if he regretted abandoning Joan. He asked if I regretted Joan's abandoning me. I told him she abandoned herself. We're the same. So he asked if I regretted abandoning Joan. I told him I abandoned me. He had enough of that and asked me how Mishti was doing. I said, "Pretty bad." He said, "I'm sorry to hear that."

I said, "Did you know that while you were boning Joan, Barry was boning Mishti?"

I was in the mood for love.

"I did know that. Joan was very proud of that arrangement."

I thought of the six of us, turned and turned around, and wondered who the seventh was, some distant minister only now climbing over the horizon to wreck us.

"Mishti will be okay, she's naturally phenomenal," I said, because I'm a very bad wingman.

"Mishti's the only one of us I respect," he said. "What the Jesus was Carlo thinking? How does anyone choose—what did he even choose?"

I wanted to follow up on that but first I had to ask why he didn't respect Joan.

"Joan liked to look at me," he said. "She found me mildly entertaining. Her name for me was Dope. Her idea of me was Statue Come to Life. I showed up at her door like a stripper. She didn't respect me either."

"Mishti loves your mind," I found myself saying.

"Mishti is the only mind I know."

"Thanks," I said.

"Mishti's pretty magnificent, isn't she," Tom said, a little more softly.

Hildegard I should have said right then *To Queens with you! Fill your heart with gladness!* I should have put on my father's mother's yenta shawl and played matchmaker, confessed every reciprocity, set the thing up, facilitated a union. But I am a wretched, minor, bloodless thing, bloodless the same as Joan, and I'd never met Nana Esther, and I'd eaten only yogurt, and I had something awful I wanted to do that afternoon and could no more feed my best friend to my ex than I could feed myself a roast chicken.

"Are you okay, Nell," he said.

"I have a bed," I said. "I have beans."

MISHTI

FIRST SIGNS OF MY NARCISSUS, SCILLA, GLORY-OF-THE-SNOW, bupleurum, larkspur. I stood in my own doorway, proud. Every bleakness had been replaced by periwinkle, byzantium, heliotrope, mauve, tea green, reseda green, mantis, and the Hooker's green that's halfway between Prussian blue and Gamboge yellow. My buzzer rang. That morning I'd finally convinced Mishti to leave the couch and come over but I never thought she'd actually do it, and now I didn't want the interruption or the witness. Mishti climbed the stairs. I thought, She'll understand. I thought, She'll even help me. I tied my hair back so as to be fully available. But then she came in crying and I found myself saying to her, "Look, everywhere, pigheaded life!" The plastic planters at our feet sang dwarf hymns to victory. I wished I could prefer creation to destruction after all. I wished there were no Barrys provoking violence in our otherwise Eden.

I told her most of the flowers were purely good, only the castor was poison. I told her she herself was our prime blossom. I told her I had an idea about using the castor poison after all, an idea about Barry, a kind of terrible idea. She walked farther into the apartment with an increasingly crazed gleam of inspiration in her eyes. Finally she sat on the floor, leaning back against the castor pot.

"Don't move," I said, "I have refreshments."

I went into the kitchen and had forgotten where I'd stored the new and unusual snacks I'd purchased for her visit. My kitchen stared at me dumbly, unaccustomed to containing anything. After a round through all cabinets, I found my Mary's Gone Crackers, my ladyfingers, my king-size Reese's, and a knife to cut both the peanut butter cup and a little goat cheese called Sonnet. I felt indisputably abundant.

"Please," I said, placing the cutting board at her feet, "it's all right, we're disgusting but we're civilized."

Mishti gulped and seemed to barf a little in her mouth. She looked at me with an expression that said, *I don't know* and *I didn't mean it* and *Fuck* and *Where did I go?*

"Here," I said, and ran back into the kitchen to fill her a glass of water.

I handed the glass to her and she waved it away. She stared at the floor as if it were receding.

"Mishti," I said, "it isn't worth all this, what's going on?"

Mishti spat some dark mucus onto my new rug.

"Hey," I said, and got on my knees beside her and leaned in to feel her forehead and saw the deep handful of dirt clawed out of the castor soil.

"Nuh—" was the sound I made.

Sweat poured from Mishti's forehead.

The ambulance said it would take a moment to get to Red Hook, that I should encourage her to vomit, to purge herself via every orifice.

THE DOCTOR WANTED TO KNOW WHOSE BABY IT HAD BEEN, AND OF course nobody could tell him. Only Mishti knew, and she lay with the blood cleaned off of her, unconscious, attached to an IV, stable. Tom sat beside her, gripping her elbow.

They gave her low-dose RhoGAM because the fetus's blood had mixed with hers and her body would soon react by producing foreign antibodies that would stay in her own blood forever. The anti-D injection would stop the hostile antibodies from forming and keep future pregnancies possible.

Tom wrote down every medicine she received: what time, what dose, what purpose. I told him he was really rising to the occasion. He looked up at me from bed level and said, "The annihilation, however temporary, of one's own personality without which there is no love."

"What love?" I said.

"I don't stand a chance with her," he said, with a very small, very mischievous smile on his face, "but she's got to give me a chance."

Mishti spasmed slightly in her sleep.

What is this instinct women have to accommodate pain?

I grew the perfect dose of a poison—does not kill, only stupefies and ravages—*Give me that*, the women round me said. We have thirsted, paid, and begged to sample toxins. Why want bad love? Joan what else is new, you were right and I got it wrong. No danger will contain its own safety. Our detox project is just for show, for prizes, it won't change the fact of the matter. Speed can't compete with intention. The bad thing must be done, and then undone, intentionally, sequentially, by a person who chooses to survive.

I look at the antiseptic toxic waste bucket filled with Mishti's shed matter. There it is, the seventh angel, and where is the eighth?

Spring in New York is so short it hardly comes. It sneaks in, a little warmth you can't deserve, an indulgence to be hidden or eaten quickly. It'll be hot soon. Then very cold again. But today, a little warmer. A little more light in the light.

In the waiting room I wipe the corners of my mouth. They are sites of constant, mysterious accumulation. It feels good to wipe them dry.

I want huge hard conviction again I want oak trees.

They say Mishti will be just fine. They say they *got her* in time. They say she's lucky to have such friends, and that a girl so beautiful is likely to have good friends. A girl so beautiful is more likely to be despised and eviscerated, but Mishti is unlikely. They called the incident unlucky, intentionally unlucky.

Joan you aren't here. I don't hold you or any place. I've appointed my rooms and exercised my limbs. I've sunned my skin with the shortest days of the year. I've smelled more than roses, and roses. I haven't forgotten you and I've left you entirely behind. I've welcomed and re-forgotten my own beauty.

The book Tom quoted was one we'd read together. Tom likes that annihilation part. I describe myself as Lampedusa described a vineyard: "ugly, mediocre, but serene and alive."

I aspire to be an old man with clean toenails.

Hildegard you were better than I could be.

Joan I've been so angry at you I forgot to bless the winter.

For those of us inclined toward scripts, here is a totally un-scripted junction.

Tom came running to the hospital from his master's defense. His thesis paper is on Mishti's bedside table. The cover sheet consists of a long title and a photograph of me looking at the unicorn.

Do you ever pee so much that your bladder flat-out hurts with relief for half an hour after you're done?

The nurses stood at a corner desk watching Tom devote himself to Mishti. He slid his hands under her neck and lifted her hair up away from her face, took a hair tie off his own wrist, and gathered hers. He pulled the blanket up to nestle her collarbone. He dragged his thumb across her forehead and unfurrowed her brow. He held the backs of his hands to a glass of ice water and then pressed them against her cheeks. He waited for her eyes.

You can find something you have no reason to resist irresistible. You can be tempted by something that won't harm you. But do you have to make appetite singular? Structurally, there can only be one ground under the temple.

They say tortellini are done when they float at the top of the water. I like to stare down into the pot and watch them when they're one inch off the bottom and only almost anywhere. That's where we are today. The hospital is eerie, awestruck, blanched.

WE

THE WALGREENS ON ASTOR PLACE FILLED MISHTI'S PRESCRIPTIONS
and I wandered with the paper bag up toward Union Square. Barry
and Carlo had sent Mishti a joint Speedy Recovery card on the
new Juniperus stationery. They had only been told that she'd
had her stomach pumped. The contact line at the top of their
letterhead listed a post-midtown post-modern Irving Place address
that promised a progressive fund, more aesthetically intelligent
and demure than its macho predecessors. I wanted to enter their
gentle office. I wanted to defile it with my own machismo.

Mishti had wanted to damage her two bodies, together, in one
go. She'd wanted her share of the punishment. Carlo, Mishti eventually conceded, had been obsessed with protection. She left the
other end of the information open. It wasn't medically or personally expedient to press her and she'd said enough.

I walked slowly through the daylight. 4th Avenue, sloth of the
East Village, made its sloping westward curve toward the park. I
turned right onto 14th Street, left onto Irving Place. The population
of Estonia exited Trader Joe's carrying rectangular prisms. A splendid dog reminded me in passing of Amanda, and I realized I'd
never see Amanda the dog again as I stopped at the Juniperus address.

A Chinese restaurant called The Cottage occupied the ground
floor of 33 Irving Place. I walked up to the window and read the
menu. I took a picture of it for Tom. The cold sesame noodles cost

only $4.95. A lunch special for $6.50. Bean Curd with Garlic Sauce! I looked up and saw a WeWork decal on the second-floor window. Juniperus rented only a room from an office share.

I didn't dare to go upstairs anymore, so I walked straight into The Cottage. I ordered the Bean Curd with Garlic Sauce. I sat at the window table. The food came quickly and I ate my brown cubes in gratitude. Mishti would need her refills by mid-afternoon. I waited. I paid. My fortune said, "Don't go there." My second fortune said, "A stone sleeping is a great force." My third fortune said, "You are a man of many abilities." At about one o'clock, perhaps the lunch bell had rung, Barry hustled out of the WeWork entrance and waited to cross the road. I knocked loudly at the inside of my window. He buttoned his coat. I leapt from my table, disturbing the tranquil waitstaff. Barry crossed.

He'd gotten a good head start on me by the time I cleared the restaurant's inner and winter doors and I ran after Barry on the sidewalk screaming, "I'M A VERY GOOD WITCH"—at first he didn't hear me so I used his name—"A GOOD WITCH BARRY"—now he turned, saw me, I yelled, "AND HERE IS MY PROPHECY"—he conspicuously speed-walked—"YOU WILL BUILD A SHIP OF ROTTEN WOOD AND BLOAT IT AND IT WILL GET VERY BIG"—Barry started earnestly sprinting away from me at this point—"AND YOU WILL SOAK IT IN ROTTEN WATERS AND IT WILL FAIL BARRY"—poor Barry—"IT WILL FAIL." We cannot remove the gross from the world but we can deny it our forgiveness. We can remove ourselves from the gross and let it wither until it's small.

After Barry crossed 17th Street, the light changed, the traffic resumed between us, he turned a corner, I couldn't see him anymore, I sat down in the middle of the sidewalk with my knees bunched up to my chest, and the New Yorkers in their solipsism and courtesy marched around me, not wanting anything to do with my distress and leaving me to my peace.

Oh Bartholomew, Oh Bart, Oh Barry the Bad, may we each get what we reach for, and may we reach for only what is ours.

I went back to The Cottage and got my coat. Nobody had stolen it. I thanked the waitstaff so much for that. A man stood outside the window now. He couldn't see me behind the glare. I put my arms in my sleeves and took a sip of water. The man outside put his hands in his pockets. Carlo exited the building and kissed him. It was a perfect, overcast day for kissing. The man put an arm around Carlo's shoulder and they walked, presumably, to lunch.

I didn't chase them; I sat back down at my table and ordered a plate of string beans. I asked Tom to join me. We'd return to the hospital together. I felt so happy for Carlo I could throw myself into a refrigerator. The death of conventional Carlo seemed to be the death of convention itself. It hadn't been love from others that fed him, it had been love from men, which until now he'd never received. Carlo's new fullness blasted 16th Street with its incandescent rays. He'd been useless to Mishti because she'd been useless to him—they'd approached each other out of common laziness. I didn't begrudge him the loan of Mishti, her unattractive perfection had revealed him to himself, and I didn't begrudge Mishti the permanent loan of Tom. It was permanent, anyone could see that.

Tom came. The waitstaff seemed relieved that I'd ended my loneliness. I smiled and let them hope. He and I sat in silence for a little while, and then there was a great deal to say.

I told him about Carlo.

"He lied to Mishti," was Tom's only response.

"He did?"

"He made Mishti think she could rely on him and she couldn't rely on him."

I wondered who we were talking about. I wondered if Tom wanted to talk about the fact that nobody except his mother Veronica had ever relied upon him for anything, and that now Veronica relied upon Harvey; that he'd never supported a single thing; that he'd even demurred from carrying heavy books home from the library, and that was why we met. What I heard Tom saying was, *I want somebody to rely on me.* What he said was, "Carlo sucked."

Mishti has never been the relying type, she's been the providing type, and even now in her weakened state, I still couldn't see what Tom had that she'd need anyway.

"You don't have much to offer," I told Tom, which was about all there was to tell him. It was also what he most needed to hear.

"Yeah. Don't tell anyone," he said. He smiled because he was about to start trying, to start offering somebody at least his whole self.

"People have become bar stools to me," I said, "I no longer speak."

YOU

YOU ASKED TO MEET AT THE BROOKLYN BOTANICAL GARDEN, WHICH
struck me as irresponsibly romantic.

We haven't spoken in about one hundred days. Silence is a
greater authority than love: you obey it, protect it, grow it as a matter of pride. You'd rather break your heart than break your rule.

So thank you for breaking. You said you have missed me. Why
is somebody missing you the most delicious possible satisfaction?
We walked into the Osborne Garden, a colonnade of crab apples.
You asked after Mishti. I told you that in Scandinavia the verb for
"to poison" is the same as the verb for "to marry." You told me the
difference is that "to marry" is a reflexive verb. I had forgotten your
life with Ragnar, your Danish history. You marry yourself, you said.
You poison another.

It's like I am rinsing a cup and turning it over to dry.

I want to take care of what we had, now that it is no longer necessary.

You recited, "Maybe for now I should just try, each day, to be a
little less than I usually am."

I said, "Ani?"

You said, "Lydia."

"Lydia."

"Lydia Davis."

My complete defeat. "I don't know her," I said.